Jewish
Latin
America

Ilan Stavans
series editor

Sun Inventions

Perfumes of Carthage

Sun Inventions

❊

Perfumes of Carthage

TWO NOVELLAS

Sun Inventions translated by Johnny Payne

Perfumes of Carthage translated by Phyllis Silverstein

TERESA PORZECANSKI

Introduction by Ilan Stavans

University of New Mexico Press
Albuquerque

First edition

Other titles available in the University of New Mexico Press
Jewish Latin America series:

The Jewish Gauchos of the Pampas by Alberto Gerchunoff

Cláper: A Novel by Alicia Freilich

The Book of Memories by Ana María Shua

The Prophet and Other Stories by Samuel Rawet

The Fragmented Life of Don Jacobo Lerner by Isaac Goldemberg

Passion, Memory, and Identity: Twentieth-Century Latin American
Jewish Women Writers, edited by Marjorie Agosín

King David's Harp: Autobiographical Essays by Jewish Latin American
Writers, edited by Stephen A. Sadow

Mestizo by Ricardo Feierstein

Library of Congress Cataloging-in-Publication Data
Porzecanski, Teresa.
[Invenciôn de los soles. English]
Sun inventions and Perfumes of Carthage : two novellas /
Teresa Porzecanski ; Sun inventions translated by Johnny Payne ;
Perfumes of Carthage translated by Phyllis Silverstein ; introduced
by Ilan Stavans.
    p. cm.
— (Jewish Latin America) ISBN 0-8263-2180-1 (alk. paper)
— ISBN 0-8263-2181-x (pbk. : alk. paper)
    1. Porzecanski, Teresa—Translations into English. I. Payne,
Johnny, 1958– II. Silverstein, Phyllis, 1948– III. Porzecanski,
Teresa. Perfumes de Cartago. English. IV. Title. V. Series.
PQ8520.26.07 A25 2000
863'.64—dc21   99-050994

For my aunt, Ana Porzecanski,
shot to death in Latvia, in 1939.

❋

Contents

Introduction

Ilan Stavans

Books talk to books about books. This became clear, yet again, a fortnight ago when a single sentence by Cyril Connolly—or better, a portion of a sentence—reminded me of Teresa Porzecanski. It starts with what has become a common belief in the aesthetics of modernism: that artists, says Connolly, are seekers of truth who help us "to attain a double-face" slant and "resolve all our dualities." Then the sentence joyfully twists and turns until it reaches a far more invigorating climax, that truth isn't single-sided; instead, it should help us to see life as both comedy and tragedy, to see the mental side of the physical and the reverse. Connolly then quotes the *fin-de-siècle* French critic Albert Thibaudet, acclaimed for his studies on Valéry, Mallarmé, and Flaubert, and it is that quote that echoed in my mind: *"la pleine logique artistique de la vision binoculaire."* What is Thibaudet really after? Connolly states: "We must learn to be at the same time objective and subjective, like Flaubert," "to have the 'double focus' which [W. H.] Auden beautifully described." Jews, of course, are naturally adept at double focus, at visions simultaneously internal and external, but Porzecanski, I'm convinced, is a special case.

Born in Uruguay in 1945, she is an anthropologist by training, influenced by Claude Lévi-Strauss, who taught us to see, among other things, the poetry of life. Add to Porzecanski's rigorous academic viewpoint the insatiable need to "do lies," as Eudora Welty once described literature, and her talent for double vision quickly unwraps itself. With an eye concurrently engaged and disconnected, inside and outside, Porzecanski forces us to see the internal life of her characters more fully, both from an objective and subjective stance.

Porzecanski's uniqueness lies in her ancestry. A descendant of immigrants from the Baltics and also from Syria, she grew up in a Montevideo home where Yiddish and Arabic were spoken, and also some German. The abundance of tongues, of *weltanschauungs*, brought along a clash of selves. The Ashkenazic and Sephardic backgrounds cohabit in her, but do so peacefully, which is, I venture to say, quite rare. (I can only think of one other example in Jewish Latin American letters where East meets West: Rosa Nissán from Mexico, author of the novels *Novia que te vea* and *Hisho que te nazca*.)

Tackling issues as diverse as racism, labor history, and Indian rituals, Porzecanski's scholarly work, most prominently her illuminating 1986 study of Jews in Uruguay, is characterized by an unpretentious approach to wisdom. Knowledge, Porzecanski seems to imply, is successful only if it makes us more humble. This is emphasized in her stories and longer narratives, in which her down-to-earth, accessible characters are seen from fallible, changing perspectives. In *Sun Inventions*, a novella first published in Stockholm in 1982, which Johnny Payne has rendered for us in a lucid English-language version, the female protagonist fulfills the quintuple roles of daughter, shopkeeper, author, teacher, and scholar in the quest for the meaning of the universe. *Perfumes of Cartage*, another novella—

Porzecanski's best work, in my view—is best described by the Yiddish phrase "*kurtz und sharf*," succinct and well-rounded. Published in 1994 and translated here by Phyllis Silverstein, the book orbits around the protagonist Lunita Mualdeb, describing the life of Sephardic Jews in the River Plata in the thirties, during the dictatorial Terra regime. Porzecanski guides us through parallel worlds, the concrete and abstract ones, and also through the illogical logic of the universe.

Porzecanski's fiction has magic at its heart, but also history and myth. Through them she searches for truth—collective, not individual. Her narrative voice is often indefinite and even ironic, a sign of her duality, and her diverse cast of characters is elastic, making room for Guarani Indians, African slaves, marranos, and self-immolating prostitutes. Critic Lois Baer Barr points out in *Recreating the Code* and elsewhere that Porzecanski's most recurrent loci are "crevices, cracks, cemeteries, unoccupied buildings, courtyard apartments, basements, and garage dumps." So the question arises: Is she a fatalist, like her co-national, the legendary chronicler of defeat Juan Carlos Onetti, to whom we owe the imaginary landscape of Santa María? My gut feeling is that she isn't; instead, she might be deemed, in an attempt to reappropriate the term from the likes of Hemingway, a "dirty realist."

In one of her essays, she argues in favor of seeing all fiction as biography, and biography as a form of geography. Maps are made to reflect not only the accidents of matter but also the accidents of the imagination, and her work is a map that combines the two. Through it we come face to face with an anthropology of the imagination. The map does not merely enhance or distort; it does both simultaneously.

I've seen Porzecanski described as the "official" Jewish writer of Uruguay; as a nonconformist, as Angel Rama once suggested; and as a postmodernist, even a minimalist, that is, a skeptic who views truth as an impossibility. I've even seen non-Jewish readers abruptly ignore her Jewishness. These descriptions ought not to become a deterrent, turning her into an obscure artist. What is most enjoyable about her is to be found elsewhere—in her multiplied self. Comedy and tragedy. Thibaudet, if not Connolly, would have been pleased.

❀

Sun Inventions

"Life, it's now known, is possible. . . "
R. Kanalestein

❉ *one* ❉

Implacable Ancestors

HOW TO MAKE an adequate distinction between the notion of silence and that sibylline noise, stubborn and chatty, filtering through the accidental chinks of leisure and pulled down by the radio receiver? And in the bedroom's dark, potently passing through the moon-striped walls, nothing shatters the insistent update, the state of time and the voices, always too muffled, of those who speak. Conjecture turns to bafflement, and bafflement to fear of what such a tirade results in. In a spasm I ask for the lamp. The manikin has trouble finding it. Somehow, against the extravagant background, distances deepen: a sparkle here, another there, the lamp keeping always out of reach. We move through the hall, unable to make out walls or doors, and yet without tripping over anything; the house expands, at will, in time. We pass through a vestige of light, maybe the vanity's mirror reflecting an ancient silhouette. A breeze grazes our skin; at times, walking, we seem to brush aside a leaf hanging in front of a face.

AT EACH BEDSIDE we touch the small warm bodies: sleep electrifies them, and if they fidget restlessly, then our children are still traveling beyond this world. The intermittent, repeated message doesn't reach them; it's still far from their brains. "By the time you hear this, man will have the following somatic features: n members, n eyes, biped, variegated intercostal fissures, pointed and cloven hooves, zoomorphism, the capacity to run-eat-devour entrails. . . . So get ready: with loved ones nearby, everything will be easier."

Halfway across the sky, the same horrible moon lulls the same people who run cross-country on watchful errands that criss-cross yet stay apart. An airtight tunnel leads us into the plane, amidst a handful of single oldsters. Somebody says: "Simple molecules, huge rhombuses, large squares . . . " and the circumnavigation begins: might there be another place to people with misery? Will other generous monsters leave us plenty of space? Is there an atmosphere that would contain us? Even now will the Universe continue to expand?

When we reach our destination and the door slides open, a beautiful landscape flawlessly, infallibly appears: sky-blue lakes reflecting a cloudless azure sky; in the distance, snowy peaks ringed by forests of every accessible vegetable green. As we descend, a horrible, fleeting thought crops up in my mind, a partial doubt, above the din of the children. When I step to the ground, my hunch is confirmed: nothing moves, all is as still as a plaster-of-Paris model in which every detail of the terraqueous landscape has been faithfully, carefully copied. We descend and gradually an embodiment occurs: our own movements become still, eternity overtakes us, not in the "beyond" but here in life, our bodies go numb, and each of us takes up a place marked out beforehand, a site the size of his or her dying vertigo, which is now nothing more than part of the scenery, so much like the planet's, similar to a fault, so alike that an alien visitor might mistake us, for instance, for live objects.

And now, look at them sitting over there: bellies prominent, smug in their small logical mediocrities, conscious of their apparent intelligence because they've discovered a vaccine for the thirteenth virus of broxilosis trepidium. But there's always something which in the end betrays them. Something exists which they don't have the spirit to distinguish with a name; which spirits them, at the age of sixty, toward the purest and most genuine terror. Tachycardia, the manner of death, the goods for the potential heirs, the drugs that stave off complaints. And another form of terror: when logic fails, when all but silence fails. Look at them over there: terrified, without crutches, without lightning rods, without swords or breastplates, defenseless in their perplexity, paradoxical in their strength, the men of this world which is yet another world, shaken and dragged to vertiginous spatial speeds, corralling the equations of their daily life.

THE DAY MY GRANDFATHER locked my grandmother and my mother in a room at the back of that lugubrious house, witches invaded our residence, clambered onto the roofs, crazed the door hinges and endlessly creaked. The first day was slow, exasperating. Huddled against rotten bedsprings, they waited for some sign to manifest itself. On the third day of insomnia and hunger, my grandmother felt the imminence of her own transformation. She began to see, through the walls, how the furniture mildewed, the solitude of that house, the chairs quiet as befuddled and slender ladies. Bit by bit her eyes began to make out winter, the narrow paths winding among banana trees naked as cadavers. And so, gradually, she caught sight of the curved horizon of Earth.

By then, she and my mother were no longer hungry. It was as if they'd learned to feed off their own innards. A peculiar satisfaction enveloped them and, at the end of the seventh day, when they heard a key stir up the viscera of the door and a cold blast of dust reached them from the endless hallway, my grandmother had already become a witch.

Not yet born, I many times imagined that final afternoon of solitary witches' Sabbath. After many evocations of it, I persuaded myself that so much evidence could only have sprung from my true recollection. In effect, I was remembering the days before, as if I'd been awaiting my future since time immemorial. And that task alone had summoned all my strength in those previous years before I myself arrived one autumn noon in my mother's ancient bedroom, among portraits of her wedding and of distant relations, the mirror witness to all the blood spilled, to all the world's pain: the bare fact, initiating the melancholy story of my reason.

Years before, in the early noon of a summer day, my grandfather had come into the dining room of his beach house, carrying a platter full of juicy oranges. Finely fat and steadily balding, he drank an herbal tea to ease digestion: "I'm going to sell the factory: they've invented some damn thing that forces me to put an end to the business." We'd all seen it coming: now there would be new flexible combs, in unheard-of colors, in every size and style that plastic made possible. My grandfather pushed away his cup and sadly shook his head. "I see destruction," my grandmother said. "A flaming cloud will tremble and make a hole in the Earth: millions will die."

As I was born, Earth pitched through windows in Hiroshima, ancient stock were demolished and transformed into tranquil-looking monsters. Cemeteries were founded, museums, monuments, a stony world to commemorate the pressurized gush of oil towers and the end of the war. Meanwhile, Virginia Mayo shook her endlessly long locks at the ardorous Gary Cooper, in a cotton field in the soft flatlands of Louisiana.

ESTEEMED MISS SOANDSO: We'd like to take this opportunity to inform you that as a result of the review of merits and demerits in connection with the call for Course Leader Professors it is our pleasure to notify you that you have been designated for said post, as of this moment, being entirely responsible for the teaching of the course, putting into practice hands-on education with all its attendant pedagogical ways and means sincerely yours I climb the pocked steps of the building's main entrance, walk for miles along the freezing hallway it's a morning in the middle of June the wind lifts my long raincoat my muffler slips free I swiftly enter the Lecture Hall look for the class roster and an empty seat I'd love a hot drink the wind has me by the knees I shiver the topic of today's class will be research and questions concerning the resources of a geographic space beginning with short-term practicum objectives but at bottom the question always gnaws at me how to accede to the thing how to pretend this reality I'm teaching is the only existing one: perhaps infinite insects I'm not even faintly conscious of are flourishing beneath the stones of the relief map's heights? And this air I breathe? Doesn't it seem as though exhaled by huge forests of which I'm abruptly ignorant? Perhaps that man in the street about to be surveyed is in short nothing more than a percentage? And besides I can always maintain that those very constructions don't exist, that the image of that place which you imagine in that time I imagine in another place and time and that my time and your time are different and the breach, the terrible breach, can't be redeemed. Professor, what's the recommended method for focusing this survey? Well, let's try to manufacture a chip that could compute as quickly as possible, we'll select determined categories we'll apply a standard questionnaire and we'll repeat repeat the new memory dictionaries, first, second, there's erudition and the crucial thing don't forget young lady that a professional should always be concise clear and simple, clear simple and concise, that is, never any ambiguous answers don't admit contradictions or opposition the third caveat is the key to locking up the Universe and shutting up yourself inside of that which you know with all assurance of being able to explain the elements by the simple movement of shifting your position inside the established scheme of things very important don't forget schemes never be vague reduce the complex to the simple and the simple to the simpler. And that's all, young lady, everything else is wordplay. Learn four or five indispensable gems, to wit: intrinsically, multinational, directed, transactionally. That's plenty. You can get any job, and without a doubt that which you most pine for: true success. Strive daily and you'll achieve miracles.

IN THOSE DAYS my grandmother shook the dust off trunks, off her silk and brocaded shawls, opened the windows of the house like wings given to soot, and bought the first television brought in as homage to this godforsaken corner of the world. We spent hours facing the intermittent light of the commercials for Valda's Pills and Paris-London, ever since the afternoon the honorable monster was switched on, after a toast of anisette. "It uses too much electricity," said my grandfather, and he retired to his room.

The next day, my grandmother organized the neighbors' first get-together. They came in pairs at first, timidly, not knowing quite how to act. Even old Laila, blind as a bat, tapped her way to the house with her cane and settled in front of the hulk, commenting—as if she could see them—on the images flattened by the diffuse afternoon light. Gradually, the screen would begin to spread inside the room, nourished by some unsuspected underground nutrient that our own pupils couldn't help but feed.

Then one night, the figures spilled out, flooding the hallways, the high ceilings, the rusty plumbing, with gray and black. The sound-belt as well splintered into a crackling report of terrified announcers' voices shouting in the house's unbreathable air. Little by little the peaceful silences of our daily breakfast ceased to exist. And we all believed we ourselves were the protagonists of a theater we were performing for invisible spectators: our dialogues were again and again scripts we'd heard, and even our gestures forgot their true significance.

"It'll be the end of all of you," my grandfather grumbled. But no one heeded the danger. Our immersion in the device had been so gradual that one fine day when my grandmother tried to close her eyes, she found herself continuing to see the same uncontrollable images. "I'm blind," she screamed, "I'm blind." "She's blind," we wailed. Enough was enough. We timidly devised a foolproof execution: by sheer force of will, in the hours when it wasn't transmitting, we burned the television on the sidewalk, beneath the banana trees and the neighbors' funereal, condescending gazes, while they said litanies for my grandmother's stormy soul. At last, the remains: among the twisted valves there lay a little pile of tiny, smoking bones. The machine had perversely digested them, perhaps as its profane and final vengeance.

The wake was long. We lit incense to drive away evil spirits. On Tuesday and Friday we boiled herbs and drank their juice, in hopes this might redeem us from such an ill-advised purchase.

I ENTER THE AMPHITHEATER and a powerful, almost milky light paralyzes me. The vast dark mass of the desk stretches out before the blackboard. I set down folders on my right, seek out a face: features—a pair of eyes, a frown—blur toward the back of the hall into expectant silhouettes; a few are simulacra of dimensions that don't exist. Our task for today is to continue with the subject initiated in the previous class, which you may or may not remember: conjugations of a problem whose development seems intermingled with the very wellsprings of the unreal, and so it's fitting to ask: what is research really about, how does one investigate, what elements are necessary to elaborate the interior structure of a thing? A face peeps out, raising the faintest murmur: Don't you think, professor ma'am, that the aspects in which the hypothesis is entwined evidence other consequences? Let's return, I answer, to the substance of the matter I explained before. Professor, ma'am, could you speak a little louder please? And you, what will you all be doing next year, next year on the 23rd of October to be more precise, at three twenty-five in the afternoon? No doubt that day, like every other, will have no implications: you'll languish, you'll die of boredom, you'll look for a way out in some scale-model of the daily round. But could you speak a little louder please, ma'am? We can't hear your voice. I turn over the pages of the outline, I finesse my way along, me, the magnanimous sorceress of the future to which you all will return in every moment of fed-up-tedium-terror, to learn at the very least to tease out the problem, just the problem.

The faces in the front row are attentive. I contemplate a pair of eyes, another, then the invisible halos suspended above them, and gradually the transformation takes place: little by little the truth overtakes me, inundating my innards, words spring like magic arranged without will or effort an arduous world is constructed light is sufficient for an interpretation, and the faces contemplating that ancient birth of Delphos sorceress augurs warlocks tortoise shells the brain's circumvolutions electric currents winding circuits. Oh! ancient Neanderthal, if you only knew, if you could witness the noncurrency of your counterfeit evolution: things have infinite ways of reverting, and coexist in lifelike, closed universes, all of them parallel. You're shut out because of irredeemable flaws, not because you couldn't construct your bridge, but because this world falls away abruptly, without continuity, without calibration or a hand's span, only a definitive end, and on the other side in another city another time, someone is being born.

So while you all breathe this indispensable air, I stay alive without a lifeline, my oxygen tanks long since spent, my earthly food fruitless as well as whatever autonomous nourishment sets matter in motion the batteries get charged and discharge with vital joy the problem's solution spontaneously appears I work out the equation $3x$ to the fourth with a tangent of 85 degrees, all multiplied by the earth's radius, and a constant, h, discovered by some deep thinker who passed for a scientist in the twenties. In the midst of this ritual a bell rings. There's a commotion among the seats. The rising hubbub interrupts the vertiginous hurricane of words. I gather my papers, exit into the hallway: this mild winter is about to be over once and for all.

THE AFTERNOON MY MOTHER DIED, Donald Duck had been unjustly tricked by his cousin, and Uncle Scrooge was intent on his search for the philosopher's stone and the elixir of eternal youth. Meanwhile, Phileas Fogg, in his London Club, bet that he would go around the world and dawn broke, catching asleep the Bedouins who carried the pouches containing supplies for the expedition to King Solomon's fabulous mines. Charlotte Brontë wept enough for two or three orphan girls, never before page 103. My own room appeared brimming over with mutilated adventurers, beautiful young ladies with wide hoop-skirts, wizened archeologists and bloody nurses who bravely crossed the battlefield. While fleeting heroes died without knowing that glory would arrive on the next page, prayers did nothing to startle the banshees who screamed about my mother.

She called out in the middle of the night, asking us to banish them: she hadn't asked them to come. My grandmother insisted on smelling salts, sat at the foot of the bed hour after hour, muttering in a strange, guttural tongue of slow and placid gesture. Sometimes the nurse perked up to acknowledge someone's presence, and called me to her side: "I won't be far," she kept saying.

The doctor put forth unintelligible diagnoses: from day to day he changed them, in the vain attempt to put his finger on the source of pain. My mother's father warned: "She's slipping away because she knows too much; now she can go over to the other side." I cried for my mother, my orphanhood mystical and beforehand. Her entire death seemed to me a feat of magic, a metamorphosis to other forms and processes, the symbol of other worlds fallen from an ancestral and already exiled paradise.

Finally the womb seals up: when all was said and done, we'd always been orphans. A few bedside illusions on Sunday afternoons, a glass of water with lily-white aspirin, a mild undercurrent of pietà through the years, someone saying "You're meant to grow and you grow." And in the blood of your first period, you look at yourself in reproach: "So I, too, can give birth; how dare I, I'm able to engender another little biped!" Is it pure chance? Or, maybe, Noah's Ark replicates itself against the visible decadence, and order erupts in your entrails without bothering to recognize that you're not perfect either and that this limitless capacity to spill a sea of life in order to see the light set in motion by a dice roll, a random occurrence maybe, never being able to predict the outcome, is dangerous. And the first time you bleed, the very humus of Earth fills your bones, you try to live as if nothing has happened, as if you were a normal, even insignificant being and had no hand in, nothing to do with, what will happen. You try to pass unremarked, let nothing betray you, let me not use my unheard-of power, let me not, after all, be the protagonist.

Your mother dies and gradually you become her: there's no getting away from it, the sequence tracks you and attracts you through every lunar month. As if beneath a curse you can't shake off, you'll sow primeval things, copy, without meaning to, hidden formulas, succumb to feelings you abhor but which are only planned hormones marching toward some final destiny unknown to you. Only through you will the mystery happen. You'll be the defender of an invisible, impossible end, you, the bare instrument of a lovable despotism, humming lullabies to your children, believing that you yourself created them. Your mother dies and you are your mother, rhythmically recreating her singular sequence. You are your mother incarnate, rummaging among her children throughout the night: you find a pair of eyes, two pairs of sufficient limbs; the color or the choler of an

organ surprises you, palpitating, and you uphold it. For this one explosive moment thousands of generations have had to weep and die,
and burn to ashes, and bury themselves in the earth your child will
walk upon, in a word, to make way.

THE NEXT TO DIE was my Uncle Boris. First he went mad for no apparent reason and began torturing the hens. The ones we could res-
cue we hid in the attic. As for the rest, he stopped feeding them,
plucked their feathers, or goaded them to fury. When Nora, his wife,
persuaded him to completely abandon his sorrowful pastime, he
began shutting himself up in his room at night to decipher his kab-
balistic conundrums. He refused all food except raw vegetables and
milk. He wouldn't eat meat or fish, but wandered about Rodó Park,
swallowing his vowels in the presence of doves. From the day he quit
his job as a buyer of women's underwear, he neglected to bathe and
the shoulders of his musty suit were permanently and pestilently
moist with sweat.

He fell dead over the breakfast table, early one morning, his attitude strangely dignified despite his state. Nora, long since accustomed to heading off searches by ominous authorities, at once
burned all his nocturnal investigations. His personal possessions,
mold-infested and tinged with rot, were donated to an asylum. All
that remained of Boris was a modest tombstone, erected exactly a
year from his death without any particular epitaph.

The house seemed quieter with people absent. A few cousins had
been whisked away on airs of adventure; older than me, they carved
out glorious destinies in distant lands. They scarcely bothered to say
good-bye to their relatives, or their deceased; they scraped together a
few pennies and off they went. The family was drained off, watered
down; the intimacy of its secret games slowly lost, its calendar forgotten. As if mourning for a past that was gradually crumbling, the elders
lamented, stubbornly deaf to reason, and took leave of themselves.

❈ two ❈
Family's End

MY FATHER HAD ME LIVING with him for a while. Aged by then, he spoke an unintelligible Spanish, and could barely see. In his house, with its grayish skylights, I spent my time discovering the indefatigable variety of grandfather clocks brought over from a distant and decrepit Europe. The innumerable canary cages in the crack-tiled inner patio covered up the gray holes in the wall. Invading dusty receptacles, I began emptying drawers full of yellowed photos out of which unknown, sepia-colored people cast me languid looks. The capricious finery, the faint smiles, a few studied poses against a background of heavy velvet curtains, shy fiancés before a mirror, naked newborns among silk cushions: all of them decidedly dead and gone, some from old age and others because their lives had coincided with planned destructions, an invasion of Germans or Russians or Latvians or whoever else, men who exerted their power over a silent, sleeping, humble village. Thus I came to understand the curious fact that all my then-living contemporaries were a mere measly frail percentage of all who had actually existed on the face of the earth. A bare statistical sample, you might say, a fleeting and diminished manifestation of all that which proclaimed itself as History, the process constructed by sweat and blood with shreds of humankind, with portions of time, with unfinished chunks of diffuse sequences. And in the final stage of wishing to know the total picture, great amorphous holes remained unfilled.

During my stay, I shook out the cushions, which had begun to breed moths; dusted the glasses for ritual wines; polished the silver candelabras and the antique spoons. In the attic, I unpacked ancient music books with worm-eaten, brittle pages; musty, wrinkled prayer books; old cartridge pens and lorgnettes. Objects, without a doubt, have a greater power to summon than acts or facts: occurrences get lost, diluted, change their meaning; someone comes along twenty years after the fact and remakes it, accommodates it to her own whim and fancy, creates his own heroes, denies the blood spilt, while objects are there with their weight and mass, taking up space, gathering new dust without changing their primeval destiny, that very one for which you used them. It's true that their endurance wears away, but much more slowly than do acts. Matter persists beyond your whimsy, your fickle and convenient interpretations. No fact truly succeeds in a given manner besides what you posit and can prove at every instant. Oh damned versatility of slippery History, they use you helter-skelter, they abuse you with impunity and time and again your only worth will be for the uses of the present, which is nothing less than the all of existence.

In those days, the old man hardly ever set foot outdoors: he collected his monthly retirement pay and some Fridays walked slowly to the temple with his shoulders hunched beneath a tattered overcoat and a gray hat, with a misshapen rim, still bearing the black band of some forgotten time of mourning. "Melej, imagine, you here," the porter invariably greeted him. My father pressed his hand and entered, dragging his feet. At seven, the winter light not yet dawned, he prayed in half-shadows, beneath the dark cupola, facing the sacred scrolls, poring over the prayer book with his dusky voice. The chorus of old men, so early in the morning, seemed to proceed from atonic reaches and their swaying intermingled with the shaking of their bodies.

"Ana," my Aunt Nora said to me one day during an inspection visit, "you must take your father to a doctor. He's feeling terrible pains of which he doesn't complain." The old man steadfastly denied my aunt's imaginings. He said his time would come without pain, asked me to bring him his cigarettes and worry myself only with being happy. I fixed my most prodigious soups for him, listened carefully to two or three doctors who reflected on the evolution and origin of the thing, but instead of ingesting medicine, he called for the notary so he could dictate his will: "I leave you the store, Ana, it's miraculous, you'll soon see."

The day he died, afternoon lengthened heavily over our shade-filled porch; the neighbor women knitted in their folding chairs; pedestrians, both the quick and the slow, may have been passing by. Summer's scent was about, and a variable calm shrouded the hours of agony: my father expired and that's the last time I laid eyes on that house. I remember the grandfather clocks had stopped, the canaries fluttered wildly in their cages, and my father's arm bore the stamped number three-five-oh-two-five-oh-one.

LET'S USE THE EXAMPLE of vegetable respiration. We have here a perfect illustration of the global process of producing an atmosphere favorable for the development of human life; that is, plants promote the fruitful usage that animals and humans make of the atmosphere. Any questions about this? You need to ask questions at the proper moment, and be sure to ask proper questions. We can only allow questions relevant within the context of our subject. Professor, why are they looking for McDean dead or alive? What is the crime he's accused of? You, Machado, always off the subject at hand. I wouldn't be surprised if you failed the questions on your midterm. Tell me something, what wanders through that mind of yours, while here we have at least forty people absorbed in the problems of the photosynthetic cycle? So then you don't know the answer, professor, you lack the barest information concerning it: McDean was born with an impardonable defect, an ominous affront to all others, an aggression hurtful to the rest of humankind; he's deaf. McDean is dangerous, dan-ger-ous. Allow me to explain the matter, professor: you could talk to him for hours, try to convince him of things, truly believe the boy has the best intentions, and when all that has happened and you think you can breathe easy, you discover that he's been shut off the whole time, that he hasn't heard you, that he's a wall or an indifferent stone. But, worse than a granite stone, more dangerous and sinister, HE IS ALIVE. You can't show him the way, predict his actions, know how to answer when he greets you, you don't hold one iota of his future in your hand. You follow me? This winds up sapping your own power, weakens you, the way Kryptonite saps Superman's powers, and, to the extent McDean reproduces himself, has children, scatters himself, there's no choice but for you to perish.

Ladies and Gentlemen, we are here to address the important topics of the Program. McDean's problems cannot affect us. Will he succumb for not knowing what his next step will be? Can he not subsist without planning for what lies just ahead? Shall he dare to disturb the life-system we represent? His very body will waste away and not even he will endure against witness-objects. Finally, we, our children, will reassume the facts and adjust them to our needs. Whether or not they pursue McDean dead or alive, know this: he has always been dead.

IMPOSSIBLE TO DIVULGE the deluge of ideas that memory spills over you full force because everything seems to have happened in some other place, some other time, with protagonists at a remove from the dialogue, and without ceremony, without hours to reveal the secret meaning of the absurd. There's now, stone over worms, late dead of afternoon, earthworms about the clean yellow bones, skeletons arranged with the strict order bodies can keep when earth remains still.

I returned to my grandmother's house; she was alone, her husband had disappeared without tracks a long time ago. We decided to re-open my father's store, make an inventory of the stock, live off the income. The day we opened the corrugated iron shutters of the single dusty display window, all the neighbor women gathered around. By the following week, they were all wearing La Confianza stockings; by the third month everyone sought counsels about medicinal herbs and had their palms read. While I packaged pins, undershirts, and buttons, my grandmother, for laughably low prices, concentrated on solving the love quandaries of the interested parties.

I dusted the shelves, ordered boxes of buttons, and dressed up the old manikin that my father used to set in the display window. It had a torso with a long neck, a look of absorption, and scant hair; the head gave way to meager shoulders and then cut abruptly to the waist. Its nonexistent legs were a rounded, sturdy stand.

I picked out, for this strange woman or man, cotton camisoles adorned with long ribbons, costume necklaces of colored glass, arabesqued silk handkerchiefs. I disguised its missing legs beneath yards of dark finery which the stand supported with unexpected grace. After all, so many other handicaps remained hidden that this one seemed to me almost a virtue, a matter of blind chance, scarcely a mutilation, which in no way diminished the total silhouette.

THE DIRECTOR INVITES ME into his office. I look around to ensure that all his diplomas are present, and take a seat. We have verified to our satisfaction that students have given very positive evaluations of your course. The tests we've conducted denote a clear enthusiasm for the subjects addressed; in all honesty, I should also tell you that concerning your pedagogical methods, things look very good. We'd like to request a meeting of professors where you could expound upon your techniques, which, in some fashion, appear to be innovative. I check my papers, I put on my glasses, I allow a prudent pause. Of course, one realizes that this sort of exchange among professors is *always* necessary, because we're *always* striving to improve our processes, what has *always* been repeatable, not only information, but the damned old formation formation formation. With great pleasure, I'm inclined, we'll have a round table, but I must stress that, at bottom, there is a limit that can't be transgressed, as much as I'd like to. It's the magic formula, it's the originary egg, it's the occult germination whose laws I've mastered but which, as a strict occultist, I can't reveal. It has to do with sensations gazes labyrinths brain transplants energy's biogenesis transferring ovules and feathers and earthworms and annual rainfall rotating the planter letting air infiltrate dirt's follicles. It has to do with storm-ridden seas, violent hurricanes, optical illusions of the odometer and one day you wake up your computer starts up you push the controls and the output is a new thing in the rough a new set of rules just scribbled on the mind and you set your hand to the task, sink your hands deeply into the task, away with fatigue, hunger, sleepiness, you invade other destinies slowly ascend difficult diagrams, throw your stubborn patience your scales the air in your bronchi into locating a new place for the old statuary which has already melted down and you are infallible unplagued by doubt because the world, more than your body, is yours. And you arrive at the much-vaunted "sixth day" and your computer works and you harness energy and in that very moment the temblor the volcanoes had rumored takes place, the terror of power, the terror and the temblor of imprinting on brains the prints of the king which is you yourself and your corona. It doesn't matter that ratiocination hasn't bothered to explain it, that the rest appears as gloomy filth compared to the shining spree of its own Sixth Day: so does the night too hide things which during the day would be illuminated. If you wish to sit on that throne there's nothing stopping you except the limits you yourself construct like interior walls; sick with insufficiency and fear you raise your own high barriers, get tangled up in history's trivia, revert your power of unpublished rule, forget it and leave it subject to the whims of each age, to anyone who takes a fancy to manipulate it, a marionette.

I ARRIVED HOME from the store tired, as if I'd had a great dream, a big siesta in the middle of a flagstoned summer way where a hammock was hung. I entered the house: in the furniture's simple order I noted the dust coating the rugs and the almost-obscured pictures leaning forward in a respectful greeting. In the solitary kitchen the grease on the dishes congealed in silence; the old icebox rumbled along frozen vegetable paths. I paused to look at the old pendulum, always keeping time behind the burnished glass. I walked into the back patio and saw the canaries dozing. Night eclipsed the windows like dank black curtains and the smell of soup hovered among my pillows. I would have liked to dampen walls, watch grow from the moist holes all of a single season's broom plant, a whole month's, pay homage to abundance. I would have liked to shake the birds so they'd sing out in that moment, making my death less obscene and, to tell the truth, less prosaic. I could have wished—I sometimes wish—to see the store burst into necktie flames, underpants burning in succulent gusts of fire, drawers full of buttons melting over the wooden shelves and the hats dispersed throughout the park for doves to use as their nests. Sometimes my uncontrolled infancy undoes the store's own memories; the rubber bands in drawers, the thread, the trim, the knitting needles, disappear without warning. I don't know, it happens, it's odd, in my memories fewer and fewer people come in to buy, I hear strange sounds from the cellar, mice pillage the bathroom. One of these mornings, when I arrive, crossing my brain's sinuous spider webs, the display racks will be demolished, the hat-pegs will pitilessly fall from the shelves, and the manikin my father used to set furtively in the window will have run away.

You come upon your memories like faint footprints, bare traces of something you're not so sure about, something permanently disappearing on the horizon, changing shape before your very eyes; you construct your past in a different form each day; it's a subtle image, a new order which, in your simile, you adorn with the necessary meanings, so you can believe that you've produced the real trajectory. You invent the process that precedes you and forget that in fact nothing anterior to the events of now has taken place. Like a spectator, you approach the thing, recreating a movable fable, another face, other faces; for you, who doubtless deserve the very best spectacle, the script is written at the very moment of its performance.

❋ *three* ❋
Witchcraft of the Tribe

AROUND THEN my Aunt Nora came to live with us, mourning her husband's death by stormy weather and years of restlessness. With her precarious bundles, and her mentally feeble son in tow, she showed up one morning and settled into the rear bedroom. "We'll do fine here, Isaac, you'll get well here." Like a stick of furniture, one more object, the ageless idiot motionlessly waited for his mother to appear, move him from his place and feed him.

My Aunt Nora was a seamstress in two or three households. She left the house early with her workbag to sew cushions and flounces in exchange for a meal. One evening she came home excited, her varicose legs trembling. "A dock-tor! I found a docktor for my Isaac. He's going to be cured."

Isaac, completely out of it, wet his bed. With her carrying him in her arms, they struck out one afternoon to see the person who would restore to him the vital light of consciousness. They returned frozen, with an abrupt silence in their throats. Aunt Nora didn't want to believe in the absurd luck which had singled her out: the sharp certainty that unjust things would never vex her child. As if forever protected by a medieval suit of light armor, impermeable to the trivial passage of human madnesses, nothing would touch him except a regular hunger, the easiest of needs to quiet, no tragedy would wrest moans from him, and without the yearning inquisition of his conscience, he'd travel light, outstripping years. What greater delight could redeem the undeserved vale of this life! Others, while he flourished, rent their flesh, immolated themselves for uncertain fates, spent their candles on negligible credos, imagined fatiguing mirages. And in the final chapters, even breath failed them.

With the passage of time, a sticky, omnipotent summer came. My grandmother began the task of shaking out each room's ancient dust by the filtered light of a timid sun. We polished the patio's flagstones, swept away all the caterpillars, opened the doors of the dark wardrobes, scrubbed mirrors indecipherably stained with yellow. Even Cousin Isaac took a turn for the better. At times the astute gaze of my late Uncle Boris seemed to glimmer in his eyes, and his legs would suddenly seem to acquire the kind of stability that lucid people require to plant their feet on this sublime terraqueous platform.

PARDON THE QUESTION, says the chemistry professor, how is it that you never consider a question badly answered? The way it looks, you take off points arbitrarily and don't compare theirs with the ideal answer, which is the correct answer.

I sip my coffee, light a cigarette: how to tell him now, without risking his death, that the correct answer doesn't exist, how affirm that which destroys the edifice he's patiently built, day in, day out on the conviction that ideas, like minerals, are forever classified in clear, strict, and ordered pigeonholes. He'll die if he doesn't know what to cling to, reel if his structure isn't closed, gets upset if his world oscillates, and if, when he opens the door, an unlikely being greets him. His computer has little space, simple pigeonholes, each thing has a one-and-only definition. His computer is in fact a wardrobe full of antique, ordered hand-me-downs. How to tell him that what really matter are only the questions: having the spectral power to ask, a gyroscope which constantly mixes up questions' parts and throws back results such as: why doesn't sonorous honeysuckle sound the indissoluble hands of? or: does foolproof honeysuckle offer up musty miniatures?

Ways of constructing a mutandis gyroscope: take dictionaries strictly approved by the Academy, cut into strips of two centimeters per concept, drop into a heat-resistant container along with two tablespoons of oozed cerebral sweat and tears and the hard-bitten wound of the left forearm, cook on a low flame stirring constantly to keep the abovementioned salve from sticking. Take from the burner place it on a steel disk propelled to spin at infinite rpm's. Follow this treatment for two weeks; when all the paste has started to evaporate begin again emitting voices: first isolated syllables such as yut ipb nko and then, slowly, invent a new language. Don't be alarmed by the initial sounds which may seem a little strange: rather, let flourish, as if you were a ventriloquist, the voices of organs. Finally, knead the perimeter, rolling it out and, from then on, a like mutation is suggested every two weeks.

Another advantage of this treatment is that it stunts the growth of peduncles in the parietal regions.

I HEARD THE MAN'S FOOTSTEPS on the porch. I saw him walk through the hallway with his heavy wooden, too-rectangular toolbox. My Aunt Nora informed me: "The pipes in the sink are clogged," and I kept on reading the ads for hair cream, the monthly bank statements, and other receipts. Afterward, the creak of the faucets and tools over the distant, accustomed street noises. All of a sudden I stand up and run to make sure the beans haven't boiled over: my aunt is kneeling on the flagstones, caressing the plumber's legs and he, leaning back against the door of the old icebox, slowly moans, his eyes closed, a pipe-wrench still dangling from one hand.

I made sure the soup wouldn't overflow from the pot, shut off the faucet, and went to the back of the house. The ants were infuriated by a geranium leaf which blocked their direct path into the yard. They'd contrived a roundabout path and overcome the inconvenience, but the extra effort had angered them. I delicately removed the leaf and they swarmed in confusion. After a long minute of meditation, they returned to their old path. I don't know if it was the dawn of a new religion or of a myth of authority for the ants, because I haven't yet stumbled on the means of reading their writing. Meanwhile, I broke up the dirt around the begonia and watered it. The leaves imperceptibly trembled and afterward were still. I fetched some fertilizer from a patio cupboard, went back, mixed it with water, and finally sprayed the whole nursery.

Around noon, I thought it better to turn off the stove so the beans wouldn't get overcooked. The kitchen was deserted. Not a trace of the plumber. The canary pecked at the remains of a rusty apple and the beans crepitated in a burbling juice, brownish and thick.

We ate lunch without any mishaps. With each spoonful, my Cousin Isaac tilted his head to one side and slowly chewed.

TO KEEP LIVING ON a single note, pitched above the tense string of urban noise, among buttons and people and undershirts—the same old unturned leaf, more than a story, or a simple common anecdote—they rigid in deathless eternity, alone in too much company, unbelievably ugly. Good day my bread my sun the count of the cold epidemic is four hundred the final delirium of the last neighbor woman the fatal twists and turns of the heart attack and sometimes even arteriosclerosis she's sick with pain and less daring than she might be. This cut in time always means one thing: space, and no amount of strength will break us out of it. Only madness remains for the artless, mortals irradiated with the much-vaunted happiness, and with griefs of sinister coordinates, invented, in a world, the details have been specified without any doubt and there's nothing on the horizon that hasn't appeared there for the millions of centuries that have gone by and that are sure to come in a single moment.

The La Confianza Store on a Sunday afternoon the corrugated iron doors shut, the surrounding houses like stage sets without walls, darkened roofs beneath black trees and the street corners askew with storm drains and always in the grocery the sausages hanging from a wire. In a lapse into madness I trot out of the house, run three blocks in a single minute and lift the metal blinds and see the manikin still smiling, grubby with dust, dirt stains on its neck and in the abrupt, cutaway thorax underneath an empty bra, dark stockings and signs that say "Everything Must Go," due to a change in season, in solvency, and with discounts of up to twenty percent and I open the dark door and in the gloom the dry dust of last light flies. On the old counter there's only a profit-and-debit register and a stray crust of stale bread and in the button drawer, the buttons, and three empty boxes without lids, and a few pins. I need people customers the old woman who pays in three installments the lady who quarreled about the stockings the boy with black shoes. Let them come now when nothing's happening and the gusts of air criss-cross on this corner in this most tranquil ignorance or peace or rather death is of the moment now. Here lie all possible dialogues, here-and-now is the point of departure through which the end is found, and the beginning is also near: the anecdote has lost its interest, the year of initiation into ranting, and the incredible attachment to name, age, and daily bread. Each moment is always only a synthesis of all that will be and all that has been and we know it because the body ages and nothing happens the anecdote offends the sense of sentences, the symbol's rigidity hampers miracles, every hallucination is ripped to shreds when we state facts and not much story and nothing exists that can resist us nothing is.

I MUST CONFESS that last Thursday I skipped class because I had trouble getting here. No, I wasn't sick, or at least if I was I didn't realize it. I'd already taken the bus to come here, I got a breezy place in the front seat, and was going along watching the landscape passing by when in a small, almost hidden alleyway, I see a huge, golden silhouette stretched out beneath a banana tree. At first I thought it was furniture thrown out, an abandoned, moth-eaten sofa, or cloth made of satin, bunched around the walk's rope railing. But then I saw it move, and before the bus pulled away, I ask the driver to stop and I get off. I find myself face to face with a beautiful lion, peacefully asleep underneath the tree. I ask myself, What could a lion be doing here at this time of day? A murmur of birds is in the air. Autumn's leaves form a tapestry around the lion's feet and the lion makes a heavy, regular snore. Its long mane is matted with leaves and shreds of bark. What this lion needs is a good bath. So I wake it by touching its back: it roars, stretches, stirs itself, I persuade it to follow me to an outdoor faucet. Reluctantly, it comes along; at last we find a faucet, rusty but working, one with good water pressure. The lion takes its place underneath, a little hunched because its back is too high for the faucet. But then the water is pouring over its back, refreshing the lion, I rub its fur and it lets me. When all the dust, the leaves, and the bark are out, I shut off the faucet. The lion shakes and shakes itself, follows me to the same corner where we'd met, and lies down again to dry. I bid it farewell. I glance at my watch and realize it's too late to make it to class. So I opt to miss a day, and go home. I hope you'll all forgive me for being absent.

But teacher, what you say is a lie, lions don't run around loose in the street nor could you bathe them, and lions aren't usually domesticated either. And atoms don't exist, or protons, or energy because you can't see them, acknowledge them, and there's no sidereal space or stardust or anti-matter or viruses because you can't bathe them. Let's agree teacher that there's only one reality and it's this: the material products we use, the chairs we sit in for instance, the blackboard where you sketch a hieroglyphic hodge-podge, and the body which excretes-eats-excretes. You can't deny biological limits or change the nature of things: a lion will always be a savage beast, a predator without the power of reason. No matter how many definitions you give, things are and continue to exist in a given manner.

Do me a favor, Mr. De Robertis, don't leave your cage unless I call you, okay? Your keeper already brought your meal at the usual time. You must understand that the staff isn't employed here to cater to your every whim. The other animals have to be kept under control too. Experiments are being performed on many of you. Each experiment sheds light on new hypotheses; in essence, the very point of the research is comparative experimentation that might open up new hypotheses.

Galileo already warned against giving exhaustive explanations drawn from models based on a single basic element, because the impetuous energy of deep knowledge can cause matter to explode in every direction: a hydrogen bomb in the desert. The recoil is total and admits no alternative. Beings, and the entire universe they constructed bit by bit, moment by moment, disintegrate in a flash, are blown into such small smithereens that they dissipate almost instantly into the cosmos. Whether, on a moral plane, this act seems aggressive, can only be answered by those who year in, year out, have gone along discreetly pretending, out of generosity, that other realities don't exist, modestly holding their peace, trying to keep inner-directed internal energy from doing them in. But in the end all they can do is let the dam burst, spray the honey and vinegar of their pumps in thick jets knowing that the founts, which in another, similar way had already exploded, will explode. And rather than to destruction, we return to the old motto that everything changes. Modifications inhere in important things, parallel and equally sound realities are set up and one circulates among them, enters or leaves at the necessary moments.

I have no idea what you're talking about. The fact that you haven't found your own lion to bathe on the corner does not imply that my lion doesn't exist. What's more, let me tell you another thing: when you're asleep, your very own bed ceases to exist; you can't prove that it does.

SUDDENLY I HAD THE IMPRESSION it had moved, its back to the ever more miraculous afternoon. It turned about lightly and for the first time I heard its hoarse, guttural, sexless voice ground between its invisible teeth:

—The counter is spattered; you should have wiped it, you know.

It was true. Dust had stuck to the glass, coating the surface with surprising regularity. The street took on the appearance of a vague landscape, a second level, out of reach. The manikin leaned again toward the window, twisting its svelte neck, and the stumps of its truncated arms, in a supple motion. Its pupils shined:

—Monday at noon a murder will be committed. Ask your grandmother and you'll see.

—Murder? I asked of it, but too late: its voice had faded into a sonorous rattle, and when I looked again, it had already hardened its muscles and fallen back into its ancient rigid stance. The unseeing look and the indifference to humans.

I shut off the light, locked the back door, and slipped on my jacket. Right before leaving, I pulled down the corrugated metal shutter, brusquely covering up the expression of the unseeing, hard, obedient manikin.

This slide shows a panorama of the construction of dwellings using materials native to the habitat, a common practice in places into which technology hasn't advanced enough to make way for a preestablished building plan using materials determined by industry. If you look closely you can make out, in the upper left-hand corner, a swallow, a member of the Hirundinidae family, with a bluish-black body. Farther up, you can contemplate the cirrus clouds of a September morning, and beyond the picture's edge, beyond the landscape, one can see the expanding sound waves coming in from very far away. Following the line of vision of a spectator looking straight on, you might perceive, if your life depended on it, the celestial orbits, and see even farther beyond, to the center of the galaxy.

Where? Where's the center of the galaxy? I don't even see the swallow.

Everyone who only sees the shack made of rushes, raise your hand. Hmm, way too many. Well, I'll tell you one thing. You haven't developed your visual capacity enough. Development requires long, valiant training of the aperture in the somatic case, and can't be taught just like that. And I'll say another thing: until you master the total horizon of the visual field, you're moving about the world practically blind. You'll have to take a cane to orient yourselves or maybe a human guide to accompany you. Even with your eyes open, you haven't yet put the capacity of sight to use: those organs are fallow, just taking up space; the sockets, empty of truth, might end up startling the very universe with their blackness.

But professor, the swallow DOESN'T EXIST in this photo. How can we see something that doesn't exist?

The very formulation of the question indicates perfectly that you're just about dead. Consult a doctor. Immediately if not sooner. Ask to be excused due to illness; don't lose a minute. Listen: isn't there a faraway world at your fingertips, one which subsists when you sleep or dream? What proofs do you have to confirm such an absurd supposition? You and reality are joined no matter what. Unless you're in it, it doesn't exist. It can only live to the extent that you construct it, keep a watch on it day and night. Each day, you yourself renew it, either as you did the day before, or otherwise. And most importantly, each of you makes a new, distinct, peculiar order. I can't enter into your order. And you can't invade mine. We live out distinct, parallel, equally viable lucubrations. The fact that we concur on a few things, that the general features are alike, that even some details are similar, is pure coincidence, a happenstance that's useless for erecting a single, all-powerful world, one that requires our daily submission. The sacred subsists within ourselves, it ends when we die. If you can't see the swallow, the swallow doesn't exist for you even if I show you thirty dead and bloody swallows. If only the shack of rushes exists for you, you'd best shut yourself inside, a prisoner, and not come out for the rest of your days.

IT WAS EARLY when I went to wake her. She was as shrunken and wrinkled as a fig. She felt her way out of bed, and listened to me. Her comment was: "So that's what the little beggar told you." I said yes, and went to make her maté. Once we two were sitting at the table at the back of the store, she ventured, huddled in her shawls:

—It's true, a crime will be committed. And soon, tonight or tomorrow at the latest.

I thought about thousands of tortured soldiers, on the verge of death, in thousands of wars, in deserts of hunger and misery. I thought about them and about this absurd, trivial crime soon to happen. Could such a disgrace be prevented? Could the much-proclaimed inevitability of events be altered? Maybe this was the instant to construct a totem, a symbol of belief, to invent a prayer capable of modifying time, of revisiting the sacred images. Reason rebels, unwilling to accept the irreversible rule of hardest fate, because its capacity to act is thereby weakened: I look out at the street and its silhouette is a mere oily mesh of gears. How to halt its noisy predestined motion, and escape, leave by one's wits? There's only the explosive vertigo of space as one is shot into the distance. But for that you must likewise risk your next breath, and with a little push you're in another, smoothly working world, but that world too is a risk.

I took a couple of good looks at the manikin. Its expression was now serious, and it wore a ridiculous black hairnet over its plaster hair: I awaited the merest confirmation of my uneasiness. Finally it came when, as I was about to close up shop, my grandmother suddenly said: "Let's hurry to the house; now it's happened."

Wild with expectancy, I run. The streets fly beneath my feet. The squares of sidewalk, luminescent, free of trash and urine, pave the way before me. Red street corners of joy, the magic of knowing the future: you run like this toward that which you know will happen, the single, sure, end of ends. You enjoy life's margins, even pain and total disintegration, carefree, because you're witnessing the sheer, autonomous transformation of matter into juices of wisdom never seen before, heaven's very alchemy on your breath.

SURE ENOUGH, when we got there, Aunt Nora, rigid, lay in the back patio full of knife wounds, leaned against a cracked vase. Not much blood had trickled from her body: she didn't seem to have much to begin with. Cousin Isaac watched us pass, laden with sheets and cares, but didn't let out a peep. Nor did he change position when they brought the coffin and the lamps for the lonely wake.

Right away we covered the mirrors, their glass too shiny, with quilts and embroidered sheets. So that spirits wouldn't upset our destinies. We arranged the six chairs in a row, assuming there would be a stream of mourners. The hulking coffin loomed in the middle of the courtyard, resting on two steel bases: a coffin with simple lines and bronze handles. Then we sat down in silence, our backs hunched, to contemplate the intricate, infinite patterns of the paving tiles.

It happens when you least expect it: you sit down on the banks of a pond and stare into it. At first you see tiny fish, slithering worms, insects hopping on the surface, and the depths of the sky sunk in the half-putrid water. That's only the beginning. Soon, that pond is the crystal ball of your past. You can see every image, the water remains still, reflecting your very thoughts. Time vanishes and twenty years are gathered in a single moment of your memory. You only have to stop breathing to know you'll return to childhood, the infancy that was you lies waiting to seize hold of you.

I see before me the rowboat rides with my Uncle Boris, I smell the wet scent of thick, green water that coats the oars with mud, the mysterious plants on the bottom, and over there, an old wooden bench on which my mother and my Aunt Nora diligently knit away. By their side is a basket full of cookies; and then, my father's legendary sayings, as he sat on the hill before a table full of household receipts. In one corner of the same pond, a photographer from the Plaza Libertad appears, his executioner's head under the dirty black cloth, getting my face and my brother's in focus, us trying our hardest to keep still, while gray pigeons compete for the wet bread underfoot. Farther down, I see a rainy afternoon, my mother playing the piano, and the aroma-taste of fried pies coming from the kitchen.

Parallel universes exist; ones you graze with your fingertips, but haven't learned to cross over into. The risk holding you back is, no doubt, that you'd vanish from the known rituals, your daily priesthood would lose its meaning and fling the threat of blame in your face. And yet, you've squandered your passage into other spheres, rejected the mystery, the possibility of going beyond the bounds that separate you at every moment from yourself; your tower, which in the beginning defended you from the other, now continually narrows the walls surrounding you. They approach, and before you know it the unlikely murder has occurred: the one committed by yourself, on yourself, the victim.

NEAR THE END of that endless nocturnal wake, my Cousin Isaac continued crunching with his head tilted to one side, and my grandmother lay there like a cardboard cutout with her arms crossed. Suddenly, there were footsteps in the passageway, and an old man appeared: a little lame, shaking as he walked, dragging his feet and cursing under his breath. He sat down next to the coffin and remained bashfully there until morning.

I thought perhaps he was a distant immigrant relation, come late to cry over his aunt once removed or his aunt's daughter, in a strange hospitable mourning. But he showed no signs of travel or remote places: an elderly man who kept his peace yet showed his grief, under the lamplight, in a courtyard eclipsed by roofs as high as they were invisible. Maybe a childhood friend of the deceased: perhaps they'd played hopscotch and hide-and-go-seek together; both of their mothers must have made them pear and apple jam together, chums, in school, on the street, in the courtyard, or maybe customers of the same shoemaker.

When the old man finally stood up to leave, I sprang my question on him.

"We weren't anything," he said. "I've never seen her before. I was passing by, I saw the lights on: I always cry at funerals."

It was his job, like that of many people, to assume the horrors and blames in our genes, without asking why, to turn pale, sever his own head, a kind of next of kin who is, finally, purer and more lyrical than the relatives themselves: crying for everyone is like crying for the species, a sense of the essence of humanity, an opaque-infinite-neutral pain for the whole unbearable condition. Roles were always there, waiting, without a first or last name, for us to fill them: a mission programmed by computers of the past whose creators, forever vanished, took with them the formula for possible mutations. So you will repeat these rites, until their original meaning breaks off or gets watered down; you won't ask for reasons or functions: after all, it was for the sake of knowledge itself that you forsook, forever, Paradise.

❊ *four* ❊

Cousin Isaac's Ascension

I BELIEVE IT HAPPENED LIKE THIS: I took my idiot cousin to the store and got him situated in an armchair up in the display window. From that post, he watched the people go by with hypnotic attention; only in his solitude next to the old manikin could he really have been mistaken for another of that ill-used species that elects to contemplate the world from a shop window. Business immediately picked up, or seemed to. At first, my grandmother and I thought it had to do with an unusual alignment of the stars; later on we figured out the truth: people dropped by on the pretext of buttons or pins, but really to look at the creature up close and console themselves, forever and always, for the other fate that had been their lot: to appear normal, move about, inwardly thanking their lucky stars, saying "I'm not like that, I'm not like that, I'm not like that, I'm not like that." Aloud, they said "Nice boy," and "You take good care of him," but their very own hidden monstrosities gnawed at their innards, played on their innocence: "What luck I'm not like that, because me, I'm better."

Others contemplated him from the sidewalk, pretending to study the prices of underwear or the hats, desperately stealing glances at the face of Isaac, a true specimen on display. There were also those who made sympathetic noises about his unlucky fate: why didn't we try a new treatment, a famous Oriental one, that had produced miraculous results in dogs and laboratory lambs; why didn't we intern him in a special institution; why didn't we sell him or raffle him off? In the face of these suggestions, my grandmother responded with a persistent frown of disgust. Then the person in question would humbly slink away.

AT LAST, the clientele got used to seeing him there like a dusty calendar and if they didn't actually stop paying him mind, they forced themselves to swallow their own incredulous fascination, and Cousin Isaac stayed in the corner, tilting like a manikin cast aside. Invariably and daily, at closing time, I transported him to the house in his wheelchair, sometimes speeding along so the incipient rain wouldn't catch him. Then we'd ascend the porch steps, three marble ones, and enter, panting, into the restorative ambiance of the kitchen. There, among the vapors of boiling alchemy, I fed him slow spoonfuls of hot tea and applesauce, the prudent nourishment that protected his mysterious stomach. Finally, I took him off to bed, waiting, in the warm darkness of the room, for him eventually to shut those lovely, too crystalline eyes. But he, indifferent to my haste, lay there quietly, perforating space with his persistent transparency. Fatigued, I'd leave the room, and in my own bed, I'd still remember his eyes open in the dark, unperturbed, his painless, groanless humanity, and I acknowledged, at bottom, the aberrant desire I shamefully hid behind my paternalistic compassion: I wanted with vehemence to be like him. I hated my own versatile, imperfect, futile means, the madness that hurtled me toward the unknown, the washed-out chaos I tried to transform into epic heroism. What I really wanted was a closed, simple, easy universe, where my every step would fall to the same beat, for the ancient placenta to slowly enfold me, suffocating my imagination.

But human beings can't, they can't, I said, looking about at the silhouettes emerging in the room's geometric space, deny their cursed capacity to create artifices, any more than living beings can deny their capacity to reproduce and make way for other beings who inherit in each chromosome the genetic vigor of motility, mutation, change. Neither can man eradicate, no matter how bothersome it becomes, his ability for incursions into other worlds, for making up new rules, establishing a different order, designing other tests, combining other data, making incursions, elaborating, conceiving, combining, inventing, discovering, always an undeniable alterity, as if it were truly the only reference point with respect to that defined by the co-ordinates of the human. Maybe you, I asked, then, choosing a face at random, an attentive look, maybe you'd like to construct an eternal place, an eternal order, hop inside and shut the door, or better yet, substitute for the door a wall just like the other three walls, so that, after an interval, you could no longer distinguish between the wall which really did have a door and the other walls which never had one? Nonetheless, despite your wishes, and no matter how hard you try for a while, in the end you'd long for your old wall or another, new one. So, you break the blocks chaotically, and it scarcely matters to you to have a hole to pass through, you rid yourself of old habits: will you leap into the abyss, or into another well-protected room like the last, from which you'll once again erase the door?

What's for sure is that there's a sequence of transfers, a series of rotations, something vibrating whose measure can't be taken, an elusive energy that sets in motion the sluice pushing forward vital liquids: a conception of otherness, like the future, imposes itself on time, in an unstoppable instance.

THUS WE LIVED FOR YEARS, three people with furniture in a dark shop, in a big house, always in twilight, the radiant noons fled, the nights always sterile without children fastened to the walls' own shadows. Our shoulders blackened by dust, our arms and torsos hardened, opacity painted on our frozen gazes, while the radio gave news of the horrors of wars remote from our understanding, a death toll of thousands who died for unjust causes or very just ones and from tuberculosis, statistics said the rate of cancer was increasing and monuments were raised in fields, crops sprouted with new mutations, antigravity would be attained at any moment and men manned the moon. But our prehistory insisted on stringing us along as it did those stubborn mummies who never finished dying, and while all this took place, our store remained in the paleolithic era, we tried out the primeval gestures of language; by accident or lucky happenstance we discovered, in two thousand years, the great and mortal fire we'd been needing.

Like a cavern, the dark store lent itself to clandestine bonfires: at night it became necessary to ward off wild animals and in the morning, we had to chase away the cold. One day we dug beneath the mosaic at three meters, fifty-five centimeters from the door and found a dead, rotting toad with one leg strapped to its body with an elastic band. In that very place, my grandmother burned macabre jujube branches and let them die out until their own odor mingled with the dust in the furniture. "Now things will change," she announced, and taking her frayed seat of willow-twigs, she sat down to wait.

SO THEN, if you've all studied, you ought to be able to draw certain conclusions: the creation myth is not a myth. Each one of us newly constructs his or her civilization out of nothing. The past is only a distorted perspective which can be molded at will, a narrow serpentine alley sloping, rising, falling, without enclosing the serene truth of what really happened outside you. What others lived. And we, always, odd, pausing for a backward look impossible yet necessary in order to believe that pillars supporting us exist. To develop the heroic tale most pleasing to us, exalt aberrations, worship anew graven fetishes. It's risky to put too much stock in our own precarious balance.

Suffer us, bah! Any excuse not to will do: a humble, more or less extensive prayer, some secret code beyond the images, a little navigation, and still one hopes this isn't the final word. In fact, it's the truth, pure truth, that business about bread and puppets. Now let us hear Venoni's dissertation. I ask above all your full attention, the most basic thing for those who wish to arrive at a certain understanding. Or rather, let's say, at methodology in brief: to hide our desire for a defenestration before the speaker's discourse begins, to not seek out the positive monstrosities in his bearing, to discover that what must be listened to is the subject at hand and not the hilarious, impassioned pronouncement of demagogic feeling, to rid oneself of the overwhelming urge to disgrace oneself, fall asleep or run away; to open one's membranes, soften one's bones and let liquids slowly penetrate them, flooding their coils, and behind, beneath the monotonous phonetic noise, let the enigmatic music of the being which exists but isn't us filter through, its frenetic dance music, homage to that other who acts as the marionette through whom we also, finally, speak. Vamoose, says Venoni, let its music begin, its horizons are expanding and an invisible perfume mingles in our tiny veins, and then, without your deciding, and while you're busy existing, the true pause of refreshment begins for us, sharp as death: that relief of not having to be, continuously.

TRUE PREHISTORY, ancient beams of legendary life, bones chattering beneath crocheted curtains, now it's time to sketch all over the walls: instead of reindeer, let serpents arise, vipers, twisted salamanders, to provoke heaven's first metamorphosis, the transformative hand of justice on the impoverished human form. We won't dig graves for those who die in the barter, we'll cremate them and their ashes will be scattered like seeds watered by a gigantic tiller whose great hands fling this tenuous fertility among the paving-stones so that what's human vanishes swept along by the curse of growing and growing into monstrosity.

SOMEONE SENT a stamp-laden letter to Isaac, asking to interview him on television. His squalid appearance, his tilted head and mute look had attracted the attention of a scientist intrigued with human avatars, the one who wished to interrogate him, evaluate his virtues and also, as usual, make him a useful member of society. How could two pious relatives like ourselves impede such a worthwhile endeavor?

So off we bore him, with the help of a taxi, to a studio both full and brutally lit. Beneath intense klieg lights he was broadcast into afternoon homes, the full front of his tilted face, the ever-astonished tic of his mouth, and the attractive, serene conformity that had seduced the scientist: Isaac would never protest, would never make the slightest complaint; that resignation, by itself, was sanctifying him.

His profound reflection impressed everyone, his internal purity, and they raved about his innate sense of things, applauded his charm, the reporters reproduced his name in the headlines of the daily paper. Like a coin of common currency, Isaac's silence served as proof of the most difficult assertions, of diverse and distant points of view. Those who squared off as bitter enemies found in this odd child indirect counsel for secret conciliation: nothing was denied, all was absolutely certain, the most nonsensical fantasies, the cruelest aberrations, all universes were given parallel approval and so, happiness seemed near. Isaac's secret was to refuse to sever the total world with an affirmation or even a concept. He simply breathed; and thereby utterly simplified the actions other men wielded like tools for constructing the future. Isaac expected nothing, yearned for nothing, lived in time's transverse section, and so was closer to life.

FOR THAT REASON the doctors had abandoned all hope of curing him, citing inalterable genetic factors, a low intelligence quotient, an atrophy of important centers of language and memory. As far as science was concerned, he was an idiot, vegetatively maintained the way a plant is watered. It was precisely this disdain of rational schemes which caused mystics to elevate his name: Isaac slowly ascended the steps of idolatry, his pale skin little by little began to reflect the souls of those who crowded around him, his clear eyes described images recognizable to those they inspired.

When at last they brought him back to the store, the transformation was confirmed: the old women knelt before his squalid shadow, murmuring to themselves, "Perform a miracle for me out of mercy, my boy." Some dared to touch him, in sinful anxiety.

Every morning we dressed and perfumed him with care, then transported him to the store, and finally hoisted him up into the display window and the timid winter light. There Isaac remained, quiet as a mouse, while the crowd pressed forward outside and the clientele quickly ascended, on the verge of breaking the display window.

IN EVERY EXAM there are rituals accomplished in the same fashion: a group of female students nervously fondles the amulets hung from their necks, or crosses the threshold of the building with the right foot. Something about these tests requires adherence to rhythms: one's very body produces nutrient cycles, the organs digest and excrete with spasmodic regularity, the beating of the blood is the tattoo of drums throbbing in our eardrums and one's breath dances to the measure of celestial music, and in the end nothing remains but to keep rhythms. The balance of time leftover until the descent, all the effort we expend in doing, in desiring, in constructing, hides the astonishing intrigue they've entangled us in; damnation underlies and surpasses all wild imaginings of asserting our will and climbing limitlessly through the stratosphere: at bottom, we do everything with the sole end of maintaining our rhythms.

Nothing is more shocking than true chaos: not discerning the weave's invisible harmony, the terror of crashing into uncertainty and of not, finally, understanding the reason for our failure. We seek, without knowing it, a rhythm for our doings, and yet, not just any rhythm: a resonant rhythm, deeply repeated, to map things out, predict them, combine, classify, explain that the first place, second place, third, fourth, are, in some way, irreversible.

In exams, the rhythms are reviewed, routines blossom like props and supports, the proven paths are trod time and again, the ones that keep the laborious brain functioning, a sequence is needed to justify acts. In each question, relationships are sought after, memory expands to fill all its boxes, past experience lubricates the order that starts the motors; freedom is no more or less than consummating a change in rhythm, without changing the order.

BECAUSE WE LET PEOPLE see Cousin Isaac, we sold more buttons at the shop than ever before: the old women knelt before him mumbling prayers, and before leaving, they cast coins at his feeble knees. This form of behavior began to gain currency among them, began to spread as if it were one of the area's most rooted traditions: not a single person failed to pay tribute to the miraculous powers of this child who day by day became more sacred, anointed by those who, under the spell of his divinity, performed an obligatory ancestral ceremony.

A confessor by vocation, my grandmother meanwhile explored the arduous paths to salvation and purity, making them visible to so many who had gone astray, and to foul-smelling old men who played the lottery with assiduous regularity. In the back room impossible loves were debated; widowhoods, vices, and deaths were wept over; deliriums flew from dusty boxes like shaken-out stockings or clothes, after long months of cramped storage, into the wincing air of reality. Oh, the cruel beauty of truths groaning in the decadent light of those afternoons: my grandmother sought something more than mere fate, a feeling or hidden reason, a plot that unraveled in the multiform chaos of facts and shed its sudden light on hard-tread paths. It was the task of great priests, and she assumed it, meekly, at her grandson's side. The gods would have no followers without such capable and persuasive ministers.

Meanwhile, the smell of incense permeated the store, marking Isaac's graceful transformation: magic burst abundantly through the door like the potent light of a noonday sun. Dignity grew about him like a body, sacredness palpitated in his gums, his look grew as opaque as that of one who only contemplates distant things, his body restricted itself to minimal movements: he was about to become a ritual object.

Then there was a final, foreseen afternoon in which Isaac, dressed in silk and with his blond head frightfully tilted, passed beyond the lavishment of this private stage-setting of choreographed secrets. Our Fathers were prayed a hundred times, again and again, miracles were invoked, and prayers to forestall the unexpected, but at the predestined hour he was seen to die painlessly in his wheelchair, his image gradually faded into an attitude, transcending the precarious weather of that day, attaining an absolute, ultraterrestrial color: one of many Christs to inaugurate, without meaning to, a new sanctuary.

The space left absent by divinity manifested itself, and the devotees outdid themselves in building the most beautiful altar imaginable: implements of offering were brought, the hollows were impregnated with ceaseless echoes, and gradually the ancient architecture, self-fertilized, began its graceful process of transformation. One morning the clear sky began to rise like an expanding bubble and a vault arched overhead, while darkness and silence descended over the ancient counter and drawers. Offerings increased without rhyme or reason, and the manikin my father had put in the display window was hoisted onto the altar. There, beneath the vault's potent light, exhibiting its absence of arms and legs, it was consecrated as the adored image, surrounded with candles, and venerated.

IN THIS FINAL CLASS I'd like to thank you for you patience and for paying attention, for the mere fact of remaining seated while I'm here and things happen, and, in brief, I'd like to take this opportunity to sum up the simple conclusion of all the subjects we studied: use the formula with care, avoid excessive ambition at all costs, return to the simple ignorance of imagination, reappraising each morning's sugary peace. Don't repeat the most common jingles, don't depend on diagrammed discussions, leave off frequenting the sultry expanses of the commonplace, the gray afternoons, cultivate all type and manner of plants, and fall silent for more or less lengthy periods, in an effort to regain the time lost in conversation, learn subtle hallucination, in short, resume some of the basic operations, letting aromas slowly filter in, dialogue with your internal organs, don't affirm absolutely or deny absolutely, live at the borders of repetitious mediocre solutions, go quietly crazy in order to enter into the fantasy of staking a claim on new universes. For the final exam don't study anything: the questions will deal with what I've just expounded on. You yourselves will grade the answers, and finally each of you will decide whether he or she has passed.

IN THOSE DAYS, the church under way, the buttons left to tend to themselves, and with divine unction finally achieved, my grandmother, the minister of so much ceremony, could live perfectly well from the offerings of the faithful. So I decided the moment had come for me to take off.

The skylights clear, the daily utensils in order, having passed the difficult diagrammed tests of faith, I packed an old bag stuffed with rubbish and took off, feeling that the past remained behind, like the most ancient of tombs, which opened from time to time to let slip out a different being, abruptly grown into adulthood, prematurely set, with perplexity, upon the sphere.

❊ *five* ❊
Totem

I WAS PRESENT at your last conference, but all the same I'd like to follow up on something you didn't say. As a way of opening the discussion, I'm going to demonstrate that you are off-base and completely in the wrong. The hierarchy of Portentus bulls cannot be denied. Like the paternalists they are, they protect all human beings and everyone recognizes them as such, by kissing their hooves and nails. They vainly twitch their tails, able leaders of any program, including those about which they know nothing. In truth, royal blood will tell in this capacity to do badly that which one doesn't know how to do.

Permit me, madam cow, to attempt once more to say that if you admit I didn't say what you said I said, then God has worked a great miracle with you: understanding is forbidden to you. You graze among hills of ingenuousness and blindness, not knowing what awaits you over the edge of the bluff. When in doubt, you attack: anything new perturbs you, the traffic and transformation of what you haven't mastered. Once in a while, you take your coat of arms out to shine and fervently hang it on the nearest tree. But rain and thunder soften your diplomas, the ink of the important signatures placidly bleaches out and runs to the ground. You conjecture about what happens, look without seeing, have your two cents to add about everything you've ever heard said, defend yourself boldly against threats provoked by anything genuine; invocations, like bombs, make rivalries explode that you can't control with your bellow, even though it's a great miracle the gods conferred on you to obstinately fend off unhappiness. It will happen thus: the stupid will inherit a virgin paradise, eternally. They'll remain within the bounds of an iron prison. Only the clean-living will be given a chance at the apple: one step more and even the door of death will stretch out like a tunnel, prolonging itself without end.

Are you suggesting that I'm stupid?

Would you know it if you were? And anyway, there always remains the final piety which unites extinct things, the egoist's desire to keep archetypes close at hand, for the structures of a half-human, half-zoological idolatry to endure, and the affability of placid offerings: a cup of tea, a little tart made with desiccated fruit, a winter afternoon in which forgiveness is mistaken for letting slide such arduous duties as those of intelligence's intrigues.

Your mediocrity is the point of closure of the old porcelain tea sets: now museums will pigeonhole your zoomorphism because you must never forget the role of beasts throughout all the great epics: sooner or later they'll be sacrificed, whether they're vain or totally devoid of vanity, to the great bearers of letters. Their blood will commemorate the ceremonies of greetings to the approaching team of prospectors: not only the lamb for its meekness, but also the very lion that has forgotten, in its euphoria, its bestial condition.

And those humans who still maintained a beast inside would boldly be cut to pieces. If something of them happened to survive, it would be a hunk of flesh, a severed member or two: a handicap more visible and meritorious, after all, than the one they now hide beneath expressions of normalcy. They'd have the aid of infinite orthopedic devices, automatic crutches to help them walk, cerebral computers would soothe their sleep until the entire race definitively perished, never again to return or prosper on the face of the Earth.

WITH MY LUGGAGE on my back I wandered for many years studying things, sometimes in excessive detail, such as the form of leaves, statues, high-sounding theories and mathematical formulas, I passed through universities, saw delirium, collected unwieldy files of useless data, read apocryphal books and legalistic books, listened to the speech of persons versed in the lingo, traveled in labyrinths, crossed enormous oceans, finally flew to the heights of snowy mountains, and despite all that time weighing on my blood, the ancestral problem relentlessly pursued me, opening to me the doors of enigmas without solutions, without rest. I was lucky if I slept four hours; in the remainder of my days I arranged my files, ideated new modes of combination and synthesis, moaned before my pure impotence and moved on to another place, fleeing from my own ideas.

In each new city I applied myself to studying the main plazas. I'd ended up forming huge folders as archives of the pertinent facts, with observations covering morning, night, noon. I included photographs from every angle, and of anonymous people, and I had transcripts of conversations I'd faithfully memorized, such as:

—No, not if you don't want to. You know what happened to Vicentina when her aunt asked her to return the ring. What a hypocrite!

—Your presence tomorrow is required. If you don't show up, I don't know what I'll do, I won't be able to stand it.

—Juan said nothing about that. I helped her because she's very old, and doesn't have the strength to wash those picture windows. . . .

HAVING EXPLORED the whole place, I had a premonition that there would at last be a final sign, some clue to indicate that the culmination of my research was near. In every town flooded with sun, sticky with flies, seated in the shade, in a plaza, I patiently awaited the moment of the miracle, as if a flower-strewn virgin were about to manifest herself, out of some impossible place, in the thicket of eucalyptus trees.

RESOLUTION five eight three one two zero one dash two three: on the occasion of the round table in which the subject of radioactive mirages was discussed, and being present the bovine Miss Whatsername, easterner, unmarried, of this city, the calflet Soandso addressed the former, employing excessively inconsiderate and aggressive terms, which don't coincide with her actual status and which endanger the merits that she has been accumulating up to now. In accordance with this, the aforementioned tribunal having gathered per said effects, resolves: to admonish with a judgment of gravest of grave faults the calflet Soandso, and this admonishment shall be tabulated in the genetophilic file, and may she, for two hundred sixty and four years from today, be the object of ostracism and shunned by the part of the bull race related by marriage to the injured bovine. Let this be published, put on file, etc.

One's intelligence would need to be hidden in better places than jewels are: it's a matter of the only true subversion. The placid, complete panorama of everything under control spills over: it opens breaches more bitter than wars and claws, shakes up crudely elaborated categories, imposes the true subtlety and grace of beauty. Oh ignored Copernicuses and Galileos, oh heretics of statism perished in bonfires of terror toward novelty: the future won't arrive; it's here, with impunity, unstoppable, and the gods of trivial credos can't fend off its advance. Stronger than you yourself, the future isn't outside you: in the quickening, programmed reproduction of your cells, the earth-shaking change is at hand, with you ignorant of your own monstrous metamorphosis, your very body, all your blood boiling over in the witches' cauldron and an ancestral alchemy creates you.

IN AN INDEFINABLE SPOT on a map, three young girls played and an old man lazily pushed a baby's stroller, while the heat rose and rose, dissolving the afternoon clouds. Then it happened just as my premonition had told me in those years of wandering: I perceived a monument in the middle of the plaza, and from a distance, I intuited that I should approach it. It was a pink, tall structure like an obelisk, and the more I shortened the distance, the better I could see it was made of granite sculpted in horizontal blocks, each squarely atop the other. At three meters, I finally made out the faces: an ancient totem of ancestors looking at me with twitching eyes, heaped up in an orderly cusp that reached toward the sky. The image of these dead blinded me, or perhaps it was only the brilliance of the sun on the stone. I would afterward remember that, while the vision of the totem lasted, silence became absolute and the three young girls had disappeared.

When I regained my bearings, I was sitting in a fir tree that threw its shade over my body in a protective manner. "Okay," I decided, "the epoch has changed; I should return to the store." No sooner had I entered the vestibule of my hotel of the moment than I heard guffaws behind me and discovered the three little girls spying on me through a half-open door of opaque crystal. When I turned brusquely around, they ran off as if they'd sighted a ghost.

Ah, return is a trap, holding out to us those sweetmeats of a dissatisfied past! The more we traverse those distances, the more other meanderings to traverse open up, our ancestors wait for us in the least expected corners, hold out a hand to us, clap their phalanges on us, appear in the midst of piercing landscapes or of untold shame like hungry, patient specters who lack the spirit to reel off their anxieties. Always on the point of telling us the key word, the very code that exemplifies you, always on the point of revealing the very meekness typical of your breed, and yet, impotent, they only offer up snippets, leftovers-remains, and groaning, we scratch at the indecipherable, we beg on our knees for a clue or a pointer, without ever being granted them.

Those whim-ridden, escapist dead are witness to the fact they can't help you: not to be satisfied, their recondite silence issues from powerful, hybrid drugs, a bottomless crack separates them from your transpiration and you must follow out this flagrant paradox until you yourself are able to cross over the crack.

. . . AND THIS COMMEMORATIVE PLAQUE shall serve to thank you for all the effort you've invested. And I'll always remember all of you. Memory isn't a mere image but rather a real movement in time, a disorder that removes us from the explosion which each new moment causes to explode in our brains. We spin out existence toward the days before and a pause hovers there before the turbulent rhythm of the hateful days to come. A soft love for what we were or believed ourselves to be overcomes us: that sweet known world, that familiarity of the already trafficked, the useless suspension of the waterfall. A picture sagely painted by us, linking us to a much-deserved eternity. Then, out of that conjunction shoot forth dissimilar lines and all waxes heterogeneous; there we part, newly estranged like strangers.

The totem must be chiseled in hard granite so its atoms can't disperse and so the genetic conjunctions endure, looped like bracelets over your extremities to carry you and carry you to so many other latitudes. One has to encrust stone in the faces of these rigid visions, embody new mineral bodies in death's immateriality, because we weren't born from a test tube but rather from a still-pusillanimous cause, from a holocaust almost, or, that is to say, an homage.

And so, in short, and so, imposing monuments are erected, on which man, in precarious efforts, wastes blood and time.

❈ *six* ❈

The Manikin's Apology

I was born like many, without expression or the capacity for movement, feeling myself really nearer to inert things than to an atonic brain exploring its limits. Oh! the prison of a brain unable to respond to the commands of intelligence! One feels, then, the genetic pull of ignominy. My upper extremities, looks, and my foreshortened body, didn't correspond to the versatility of my galloping thought. Without legs, I couldn't change my position in space precisely either.

Sunk in my affliction, I nourished my body, for years, only on the most timid desires, later on unconfessable, omnipotent impulses which demolished the energy reverberating among the gears of thought. Until, sick with desperation, always standing bolt upright, having changed owners, I arrived at this final store. A man, spare of body, received me with fraternal warmth, dusted off the parasites gnawing and burning me, polished my various parts and finally gave me a place, a place I could call mine, in the display window.

In the idle hours he spoke to me of the days of his youth, his feverish dreams, told about a long voyage crossing intrepid oceans, about years he spent selling newspapers and candy in exchange for a meal, about his gradual consummation as an inventor of sayings and proverbs, which he pontificated every afternoon with profound sincerity.

And so, finally, my capacity for thought was nurtured by a content befitting it; I no longer lamented my rigidity and inertia. Others, more human, seemed to have always been more inert than I myself; the talent for versatility and the sharp propellers that might have given them flight were checked by fear and laziness; their own dormancy seemed fetid to me, as if putrefaction had set in long before death.

Your father was the one who loosened the reins on my true movement, and at last freed the prison of flesh—for me, wood, for others, flesh— granting me knowledge of other probable universes sparkling, simply wait- ing for my consciousness to touch them. Without a diving-suit or space-suit I could now explore those worlds, and I needn't abandon my place in the display window to do so: your father finally taught me true witchcraft—it was incomprehensible to others, this willingness to risk sabotaging one's vir- gin lucidity, then save it, never losing or delegating it. It's the only freedom that exists: letting go of mediocrity, of the impulse to keep eating your an- tediluvian fat, to keep nourishing your cells, which will verily perish, verily perish when the clock, as was foreseen, winds down.

WE WERE FRIENDS during those last years, friends of few words: this laconic streak representing an implicit, underlying agreement, a con- formity beyond anecdote and dialogue. We were comforting com- panions to each other, loyal to a fault, good pals. I don't know if you all are aware that dogs are more loyal than humans, but even more so than dogs are these impartial, genuine, thinking beings called manikins.

I'd returned unsatisfied from my travels; all they'd done was awaken in me trivial intrigues and restlessness, innocuous vanities, and an underlying hunger gnawed at me.

I returned to my manikin as to the being I most cherished, who, despite all my sins, received me with no questions asked, with open and ever-understanding stumps. It could love mankind all the better because it wasn't a man.

Inured as it was to repeated disillusionments, the place occupied by the manikin fascinated me: on the margins of the world, behind the display window, was the very place which granted it the lucid peace I yearned for.

What vanity of will had dragged me on a goose chase through the sinuous byways of consciousness, what blind ambitions had made me imagine fires where they didn't exist, and that I was the acclaimed, undisputed heroine of such vast libertinage? I'd taken the wrong path: I'd concocted the idea that "in the image and likeness" meant "exactly the same," and fearlessly instilled with the power of the gods, I'd aspired to a sorry imitation, an aberrant excrescence, the awfulest of offal. That is why I'd now returned, handicapped, like my manikin but still less enlightened, to occupy the other seat in the window: those who pretend to the sacred and are not given divine talents will forever drag themselves over the dust.

WHEN I GOT OUT of the taxi, the door was open and the breeze blew through from the alley. I paid the man and remained standing on the walk, looking at the familiar façades. With an effort, I plunged into that contrite jungle. The dining room seemed dark, the pieces of furniture vigilant at their ancient posts, the crystal trays empty. But the grandfather clock continued to tick, echoing oddly in the silence.

I began searching for the old lady, room by room. I burst through doors, inspected beneath beds, and even looked in the wardrobes. I went out onto the patio, hoping against hope, but all the tiles were empty of her. Like the canaries, the worms, the moths, she'd disappeared and nothing remained behind except her palpitating, rotund absence, the absurd paraphernalia of terraqueous life pregnant with

it, a continuous, pulsing, mobile acceleration of it in the early darkness spreading and spreading backward through that empty house,
toward old times. Those who know something of themselves, allow
themselves the luxury of disappearing in this way, in a humanitarian
act of magic, while their nocturnal lives continue, extant in the construction of all enigmas.

I run at once to La Confianza Store: the front room bare, full of
cobwebs, the glass smeared, looking like a picture window colored a
strange and burnished gray, the back room a black hole with the ran-
cid stench of brown rats. Not a hat peg, nothing. Suddenly, a stiff,
armless shadow comes up beside me. I turn around and see it existing
there: naked, on its old stand, the manikin my father placed in the
display window to model lovely camisoles.

—*Where are you in your research?*—it asks me in a disguised voice,
out of the depths of its stuffing.

I explain to it the principles and stages of the matter, the necessity
of making plain the irrationality of the situation.

—*Your search has no end; you can never finish*—it answers.

I insist on explaining to it patiently all I've gone through, the
paths I've followed, the evidence I can produce.

—*If you insist on proceeding, you will suffer. You'll fall seriously ill.
Cease while there's still time*—it replies.

Imperturbable, I show it some of the results I've obtained, some of
the photographs I've filed away, the conversations I transcribed
through so many uncertain years. And I open the front door. I think
that it needs air, that I need air. I push its stand to the door, on the
threshold where it can view the street. I suppose it sees what I see: a
lively morning in the neighborhood, people scurrying about, the
clink of glasses and silverware indicating the approach of lunchtime.
One must eat, break one's fast, perform afterward the excretory functions, and later on sleep and initiate the cycle anew. Doesn't it see

that? Or is it playing dumb? Or maybe it has forgotten to land in distress upon the stones?

MISS SOANDSO by means of this memo it is our pleasure to invite you to participate in the Latin American Salamander Seminar, conferring on you the presentation of a dissertation on the subject "toward a work methodology and perspectives" we appreciate your RSVP ASAP we are sending you a plane ticket for your transport to this locale we look forward in advance to your disinterested participation. I, my arms full of books, lean against the back of a cushy, comfortable chair and while the smiling stewardesses in the aisle feed me to excess, while ladies and gentlemen, some sullen, others hotheaded and less youthful, with unbrushed hair and aggressive looks about them, and pious, silent nuns, and tortuous geriatrics with amphibious grandchildren, together make a turbulent murmur which expands along the cabin's unbreathable surface. Among the air conditioning and torpid expressions and tourist maps, I remain sunk in a too-difficult, even grave task: I forfeited my own wish to be diffuse and vague over my lunchtime glass of white wine, struggled against my desire to walk up and down the aisle commenting on the avatars and changes in altitude of our voyage, sacrificed my serenity on a task unknown to the rest. By the sheer effort of my mind, I held the plane aloft in flight. If I stopped doing it for even an instant, the plane would fall, the terrified people wouldn't have time to be surprised, the subtle balance that bound my consciousness to the regular throb of that potent machine was sealed by the coincidence that I had chosen, on that day, that plane, at five in the afternoon. In case you all didn't know it, on account of your being young and not having rolled it over in your minds much, on each and every flight made over this incredible sphere, someone always holds the plane aloft by sheer will, controls the laws of gravity, keeps the plane on its route, and that person is the true pilot. Her certainty orients her toward the goal, and even if some parts are left to chance, say some imperfection not foreseen by the computer, the true pilot, incognito among the passengers, hidden in the guise of a normal tourist, acts as a compass: the needle points north. She can't get lost. Keeping the flight firmly on the track is an exercise in divine will, is the continuation of the balance that should also sustain us here, on Earth.

—*Think about it*—the manikin says to me with its sexless voice, as it disapprovingly watches me eat. The last few months have been a little difficult. It hides from me in my moments of greatest trial, but will suddenly appear behind a window blind, behind a half-open door, or a mirror, like a mysterious spy who is tailing me.

I've tried talking to it, persuading it, I've tried clarifying human errors for it. But it always ends up bursting out in an intermittent guffaw, while its mouth stays motionless, contemptuous.

—*Think about it*—the manikin constantly repeats.—*I wouldn't advise it: If I were you, I wouldn't do it. . . .*

I manage to understand its erect posture better; it's not so much there incarnate, but rather issues out of my own soul, out of that damned aberrant essence, out of that object which is me, constructing the illusion of an exuberant joy. The manikin is I myself, or selfsame me, an integral part of one of the other subterranean dimensions: simply a path for a more distant ego, obliterated, unsuited. And in conversation, the conversation has been this long expiatory monologue, this exorcism of being without contiguities, this mutilation of heaven, here and now.

—*What you wish is to discover the originary egg, the great mystery of being and of matter, and that is forbidden you. After all, who do you think you are? What vanities do you think up and ascribe to yourself? What power do you seek, to make you wish to possess that which isn't yours nor ever will be so long as you live? Think, if you still can think: why are sanctuaries silent, their tranquillity never disturbed?*

Its prepotent invitation for my conscience to agonize had upset me. How could I quiet my doubts, how leave off seeking, making incursions, gathering data, and return to a belief in the trivial consolation of an uncertain, coincidental order? How achieve a definitive passivity, renounce forbidden fruit, and at last be enveloped, for the rest of my orphan life, in the simple darkness of the given?

LADIES AND GENTLEMEN, professionals and colleagues, meritorious professors and eminent sirs: I didn't prepare my lecture and I most deeply beg your pardon. The truth is, I didn't think it was necessary to take up minutes and hours of your time to regale you with fancy combinations of language. There is one sole argument in my favor: not a single thing can be affirmed concerning your preoccupations, and anyone who puts his two cents in to the contrary, I can assure you, is lying, catastrophically lying. Space must be left for intelligent silence, the howls of a sham, infirm intellect must be suppressed, a thoughtful evaluation of circumstances conjugated, and the old, yearned-for paradise made sure of. The processes already under way need to be revitalized: if the end is important, return to the beginning, evoke the lost deities, contemplate with large pupils the laborious orbit of the planets, offer up offerings, ritualism is more pertinent than facts. To step outside the lies of history, a deep vortex is needed, which, buried in the blizzard of these pendular universes, establishes the moments of entry and exit, the subtle impulse allowing us to instantly travel at the speed of infinity. Oh! the celestial spin of all the cohort of galaxies breathing and beating in the gases of the vital liquid: about them there are no assertions. Manifold worlds trail your tracks, wait for you in a corner, they know before you that the joy of joys is right in your vertebrae, delicately engraved with the faces of implacable ancestors who adorn you and transport you and engender you every day with precise codes, exact information, the plan agreed on: everything wheels about you and you, all the same, construct each of your worlds, out of humus into cirrus, tenant of an intelligent ancestral inn.

I didn't prepare my lecture because I realized I have nothing to say. . . .

❋ *seven* ❋

Sun Inventions

WHAT'S NEEDED FIRST is an epigram and the coming forth of the lap in which the prodigy will be nourished. The epigram should be stuffed with arduous dawns, nights of insomnia, the body thrashed in desolate pastures, questions heaped up in icy caverns and ceaseless conjectures should take place in every language and when no answer appears, the womb begins to swell, barely perceptible spasms commence, there is a slow and steady beat. Second, read like there is no tomorrow, forget about punctuation, be open to all the forbidden influences, drink in the proper potions. Third, contemplate the belly's expansion, its ominous autonomy. Nine months later, along with guts, dust, and blood, endure the emergence of a tiny, brilliant sun, pluperfect and shining from kilometers away. When you try to take it in your arms, you confirm to your horror that it burns, that it is capable of incinerating even its very progenitor. So set it free, watch it fly, climb to reflect terrestrial waves, keep its heat, be the sum of the shines that the species will later need.

As might be imagined, sun inventions required unheard-of gumption: given that the shining is nourished in one's own guts, this re-splendence can also blacken ashes and if the membranes aren't tough enough, they'll yield only a crematory dust. On the other hand, those who risk holding in the brilliance and facing the ardor of close con-tact will invent a thousand igneous suns. Beating drums, they'll see them rise up like emblems in which the genes themselves remain in-tact against any spurious witchcraft, to illuminate this black and icy hole in space.

Faced with the mystery of these pyrospheres, an opulent heroism takes heart in the darkness of the human womb, because nothing ex-ists until light ignites essence and reveals matter. Such designs re-quire defiance of our flames, the imminent creation of bones, an an-cient irreverent destruction, in the hope of later shedding light on at least a detail, or maybe some trivial, less obvious aspect. Oh Lucifer-ian epics, hecatombs provoked by hell's own effervescence, giant bonfires that consume and construct perennial matter, devils who feed on you yourself when you invent suns, when you lust after the corrupt power of distinctive light, they're nothing more or less than the only possibility for distinguishing colors, choosing a form in the context of doubt, seeing, in short, that differentiation of the primeval thing.

And if no one invents suns, in the worshipped orbits of space, nothing exists. And if no one feeds the suns, nothing will survive. Conscience itself will lose its consistency, little by little disintegrate until it is sunk in the mossy, blank blackness of indifference.

And if no one invents suns, you yourself won't be created.

❊ *eight* ❊
Emendations of Preceding Chapters

WHERE IT SAYS A it should have said B. Any coincidence with reality is nothing but a coincidence. Where it said he desired me it should have said there were moments of color-choler we had our moments. Where it says they knew not what they did forgive them Lord justice is sometimes forgiveness and sometimes vengeance and so the totem is surely larger it lengthens it's a matter of congenital heredity a limitless feat without any alternative. Vengeance always snuffs out those seeking revenge. Justice only draws strength from the just. Where it says page five, it should have told the precise formula for logarithm x, the variation carries over a variable series which can be found in the table for plenipotentiary values and appended indices. Or really, it should say in agony I stop this macabre flow and the typewriter ribbon smiles and tells me stop Teres stop girl stop. Results obtained: the program ninety-nine percent complete but there's always that one, always that remainder, you'll never learn to account for that one percent, a stretchy hunk of chewing gum, other circuits will cover the unspeakable: if p is true then q is false and so it should have said suppress chapter one, two, suppress the whole book: it's better to take a chance on the abyss than on trumped-up fullness.

It should have limited itself to strictly important things, the most notorious, and not the chinks of what it wished to be, but in the same way painters destroy the faithful photograph of the autumn trees as they truly appear, it's imperative to break forever with the anecdote tainted with lies, also break with form—syntax and punctuation only remain for spent categorical assertions—and words themselves, which have much greater force than facts because without question they induce them, should rest free of logical connections, with their force intact, intact and unlifelike; more so than facts themselves, words, resonant, invoking actions, leading on the naive, and flowery demagoguery is tricky and slick without restraint on the abstract horizon of dogma. That is why an eye must be kept on them. Yes, outside the aberrant chains of rhetorical mediocrity, they could be unleashed onto their own paths, making a new order of language, breaking for good with the image, constructing universes worthy of nascent existence. Exclusive word-vehicles to carry us beyond the apparent practical ends of solid matter, of that graven concretism worshipped in temples, of that reality taken for the only one and that illusion of being we dearly wish will solidify into mineral rock, set in taxonomic stone for the future centuries still to come to us.

It should have said: words will have their way, isolated from their smelly meanings, they get mixed up on purpose, every alloy of strict fixed signification demolished them, new dictionaries are prescribed for them, zigzag flotation in brains to bathe them in exact logic so they'll function properly. It's verboten for them to order themselves, come together, coordinate, coordination being contrary to the essence of new universes. It should have said that license on open letters, which is the same as saying, license to open up concepts, doesn't commit us to anything more than the dignity of medieval moralism. From now on, words and not acts or facts, words laborious warps, profane, holy, to redeem the horrific sin of acts, words dancing rock or boogie-woogie, a light-footed charleston, a mazurka, a melodious rhythm to wear away the hard lines of facts, the way incessant precipitation erodes the edges of precipices.

Where it says "the dead shall be buried" it should also say, let new lives be conceived, let the alchemical liquids be mixed with care, leaving aside recipes that don't do the trick.

Where it says good intentions are enough, it should have said enough of good intentions, enough, it's not enough, it should have said what it will take is the total extirpation of any and all intentions about the whole ambivalent project: good today, bad tomorrow. In short, eradicate the whole network of ambiguous projections and be left with the bare control of innocence, bravery, heroism when innocence is over, and the harmony of stray threads. Leave behind all blood, all emblems, the entire existence of fallible desires and consolations after the fact: only what is sacred merits the gods' investiture; the rest, daily vulgarity, a ghost at best.

Concerning the errors, cut them up and stick them in an album, then raffle it off, and if you're lucky, you'll be the lucky owner of a folding submarine bicycle that will fit in the trunk of your car, will retire between four in the afternoon and eight in the evening to the canal with your first and last name and all your updated ID info, and a free-floating inconsistent emotional sense, a sickly, spastic psyche in full hilarity, you'll trot out the anecdote with strict rationality, get inspired by a couple of sure influences, so that individual wingbeats won't evoke mythic idols, after that, it's careful typing, reserve a box seat to watch the spectacle: sign autographs in accordance with the theatrical production, invite a group of distant, half-forgotten kin, model fashions that match the living-room rug, file out of your enclosure and watch the results.

It should have said what it doesn't say but that isn't to be grasped within the macabre limits of a plain alphabet. Rest assured, then, that the true book is absent, the complement, call it, the would-be, the one that is not written nor ever will be.

Epilogue I

I WOKE UP on a cold tile floor. A patio of high roofs, in which the past didn't exist. I sought my body and, as if from far away, I made out two small, oval hands. I wanted to keep finding out about the rest of my face and body: I had a faint intuition that I should leave off looking for them. I dragged myself as best I could toward some opening, and had the vague idea, as I did so, of having seen this type of house before.

Nearing the point of light, I found a room with two reddish stools and a matching table, on a square, deep maroon floor, surrounded by stones spattered with old, dried-out ointment. I stopped; I studied the walls keenly and afresh, and at last understood: all was blood there, dried blood, washed up, the blood of millennia in infinite strata covering the stones, the floor, the ceiling. That on the table was still fresh.

Oh true altar of pagan cults, sought by a thousand men in a thousand apocryphal forms, I was about to discover the infinite possibility of knowing myself, of stepping outside myself in order to see myself, of traveling through asymmetrical galaxies without having the deformative law of gravity, channeled through the human, slip out of my grasp. I was going to contemplate Earth, at last, from a great distance: the ceremonious solar system, to a cadenced rhythm, would follow in my footsteps, measured and affable, and little by little, a drop of affection for my tired feet, my poor hunger, my trivial sleep and waking, would penetrate me.

Only in this way could they be cared for: when, from a great distance, they could be apprehended whole, when the most global of reaches made them blur together. Then, a faint pity would start to penetrate you as if you had, with conviction, let go the warp of all vessels and, without sacrificing their fluidity, without checking their energy, ceaselessly removed their distances and altered their remote reaches. To love humans, you must definitively cease to be one of them.

Epilogue II

—I'D LIKE TO KNOW what you're putting in that damned book you're writing.

—Well, I . . .

—I'll tell you: you should first write something about your parents, the education you've been given, and all the sacrifices it implies. In short, begin, maybe, with your maternal grandparents. Explain how they crossed the Atlantic, hidden as stowaways on a boat. From Beirut to America. How they said good-bye once and for all to their parents, who they never knew if they'd see again.

—You should also write about your other grandfather, because the paternal side is just as important. Say, for example, that he was born on the shores of the Baltic Sea, and was the owner of a big sawmill.

—You should also tell, in great detail, the story of the ship they mistakenly arrived on in the United States. How there were no immigration permits there to be had, and how they traveled along the coast of South America, from country to country, until they finally disembarked in Montevideo.

—Because, how interesting will a book be that doesn't tell the past of your ancestors, who didn't have the time or leisure to sit down and write? Because they didn't have the advantages you now have either, to contemplate the world while they serve you your meals.

—I don't think you should pressure the girl like that. Instead, leave her with no strings attached. Let her write what she wants. If the past interests her, then let her write about the past. If she doesn't want to tell family histories, she shouldn't tell histories. Anyway, history is on its way out.

—What do you mean?

—What I say. History is decidedly just somebody's opinion. Nobody can ever climb into the skin of those who were her ancestors, or into her children's skin, in the future.

—Well then, she can write about her friends. But I'm afraid she'll be hard on us, making us out worse than we were. We, who nourished her in our bosom.

—She owes us many favors.

—We're not so bad.

—Or so crude.

—She can't take revenge like this.

—The problem is if the book gets a lot of attention. What would happen if everybody found out what we're like, our intimate lives? We'd be the talk of towns. Wide distribution isn't a problem in and of itself, but that everybody would come to know so much and so well, is disturbing.

—So, it's better to persuade her not to publish the book. Tell her that later would be better. Give her pause to think and maybe even change her mind.

—Sure, we can convince her to take up another hobby: watering plants, collecting stamps. That would be that.

—She's always liked to paint.

—Too bad she's so mediocre at it.

—And after all, why, I wonder, does she have to write? She's a mother, has children, works, what more could she want?

—I've asked myself the same question. Why can't she be like everybody else? Why can't she be happy the way she is? If she didn't have anything to eat, I'll bet she'd worry her head with truly important things.

—She's still young. She'll grow up. I have a premonition this is her last book.

—Last book? How do you know?

—Yesterday she was acting strange. She said her brain hurt. She said she'd finally rid herself of the weight pressing down on her.

—You think she meant she'd finished the book?

—She said she couldn't finish it because these books are never finished. She said she simply interrupted it, left it incomplete.

—She said those exact words?

—Yes.

—Then it must be true. Maybe she's going to quit writing. She interrupts it, but if the book has no end, she's not going to keep writing.

—It's better for her.

—Better for everyone. She doesn't really write about the things and people she should write about. If the truth be told, she digresses. She doesn't keep her eye on concrete things. I think that's her chief defect.

—What are you two murmuring so much about? You're going to wake her. The doctor said she should sleep for at least twelve hours.

—Did it wear her out that much? How can somebody get so worn out by writing a little book?

—Well, she hardly ate. You had to insist two or three times before she'd eat.

—No, you two don't understand. She just wasn't hungry. A person can live ten or fifteen days without feeling hungry. It's normal.

—But where did she get the energy to write until three in the morning?

—She's like a battery. She recharges herself.

—But that's unheard of.

—Doesn't ring true.

—Impossible.

—The girl is sick, but in the head.

—She was always crazy.

—All artists end up like this.

—Not all. Some make money, come into their own, throw everything out the window, and live it up. Why couldn't she do the same? Let her be sociable, get some sun. Why should a person have this mania for seeming dramatic?

—It's getting late, we have to go.

—It's all right. Let her sleep.

—Who's coming to make her breakfast tomorrow?

—I'll come.

—No, me.

—Or me.

—We'll all come. She might decide to get up.

❋

Perfumes of Carthage

※ *one* ※

THOSE WERE DREAM LANDS, thought Lunita Mualdeb more than thirty years later. Her blouse clung to her damp breasts and her computer screen winked ironically at the lines of a notice from the Accounts Receivable Department. User number seven hundred thirty thousand, eight hundred and ninety-two would no doubt curse the warning that read: *Once the time limit has expired for payment of the tax, your property will become subject to fines and seizure according to the appropriate article of the regulations currently in effect.* Sultry air floated up four floors and into the window of the office she shared with two other civil servants. At Carnival time Avenue 18 de Julio teemed with vendors and strollers, beggars and idlers. It was the end of an extremely long, warm, and uneventful day.

Not lands, but worlds, she said to herself and looked from side to side. On her left, the boy with thick glasses had vanished, swallowed up by the hallway. On her right, the gray-haired woman was poring over some forms while chatting amiably on the telephone. Her voice, cut off by interjections from the other end of the line, disappeared into the noisy air of the gaping window. With a slight gesture of annoyance, Lunita sat up, stretched her legs, and smoothed the skirt over her hips. Then she walked to the window and stuck out her rounded bosom. At the height of such afternoons the breeze was so soft and sticky it felt like steam. Below, one could see wooden chairs organized in parallel rows along the sidewalks, waiting impassively for the prolegomena of a parade that was about to begin. Small children were already on the loose, chasing one another in circles. Elderly women with canes had started to sit down.

The sight of them stirred old memories. She envisioned her great-grandmothers floating like nymphs through perfumed gardens—and the images kindled a realization: they had performed miracles, feats of magic. All of a sudden the world seemed strange and unfamiliar. Noiselessly, one of Lunita's sighs rose through the air, zigzagging in its ascent. Approaching clouds that seemed to take shape right in front of her eyes stood watch. Now forty-four years old, she examined the palms of her hands as though trying to discern their form and design: inextricable lines traversed them in each and every direction.

Tangled lives, Nazira would have said, if she were to see them. And perhaps she was seeing them—who could say?—seeing the broad, reddened palms, and pale backs with grooved skin stretched between ridges of lifeless bone. Hands that rubbed one another, consoling, cauterizing themselves. Hands that once belonged to aunts and to aunts' sisters, and now, mysteriously part of her, they sprouted from a hidden root.

The music of a trumpet, small and mocking, began to come in through the window. Below, the din grew louder. Vendors selling masks and sweets had invaded the corners and pedestrians were squeezing past tables in the street. Lunita Mualdeb hid her hands and crossed her arms over the effervescent avenue. She realized, as though someone had undertaken to show her, that lives like those of her grandmothers and grandmothers' sisters would never happen again. The present was prosaic, lacking delirium, she thought. And people walked home at the end of the day, without illusions, without passion. All that oriental splendor had drained away in a dizzying vortex, stripped of love by the immediacy of hard facts.

Those were dream lands, countries that weren't countries but worlds, she told herself. Her great-grandmothers had constructed sacred, ineffable substances. They performed miracles, feats of magic. She realized, as though some force were actually showing her, that such lives would never happen again. Hastily searching through her skirt pocket, she felt the cold bronze of an elongated key. With its touch the image of a huge dilapidated door—looming over a deserted street in the morning—seemed to emerge from heaven's navel and move toward her. A shabby façade bowed in her direction.

I never really managed to learn anything about that family, she said to herself as she contemplated the river of people below. There were hundreds of relatives. And I never met most of them. With each story, their profiles changed. All I can say is that they loved and hated passionately. And that they were definitive beings. Swarming, prowling, circulating through what appeared to be a tribal recomposition, they were born of one another, some piled on top of others, and invented the same sayings, the same farces. The stories gave birth to one another in strange combinations, as though they had lives of their own. Tales told throughout the generations, each one accumulating details, characters.

Radiant places I can no longer remember, disappearing façades, balconies. Certain patios penetrated by a distinct sun. Traces remain, of course: deceased neighbors stop me to ask about my ancestors. And what have they done with that dress Lidia wore to her daughter Alcira's wedding? Whatever happened to the bronze *narguile* Nazira used to smoke? Apparently someone saw it in an antique store. And what about those bottles filled with the intense aroma of gillyflowers and violets? And the brooches set with iridescent glass stones, brooches preserving long strands of hair, still wavy from heavy braids? There was an oval mirror with a lacquered handle that projected my face as it should have been: a face that told the histories recounted by each one of those relatives during the languid after-dinner conversations of summer.

Now all I see is a family woven backwards, like an Adamic genealogy unfolding slowly before my eyes. Shackled to a line that should have disappeared, I write letters to ghosts. I weep. I could have stayed in the wombs of those women who made unleavened bread. Never to have arrived through some twist of fate—an orangutan stuck his quasi-human face through the bushes of a steppe and left the mark of his five pedestrian toes in an atavistic garden—nor through the seed of suffering.

Suddenly huge painted papier-mâché heads came into view. Monsters with faces contracted in perpetual smiles. Blind eyes. Beneath bodies made of cloth, pairs of human legs danced comical steps for the long lines of children. From behind them came the clanging of black drums, like some secret terrestrial heartbeat that could split the night air and suffocate you. Lunita Mualdeb turned her back to the window. The office was deserted. A warm breeze opened the files and shuffled the records. Orphaned papers flew through the heavy air, and the whole place turned into a cesspool of ancient artifacts that refused to disappear.

✳ two ✳

IN HER DEATH AGONY—which lasted no more than an instant or two—Nazira Mualdeb reviewed the months preceding her granddaughter Alcira's wedding and a torrent of ghostly images spontaneously abandoned its place of forgetfulness to rise up and impugn the toilsome miseries of her life. From the dining room, Lunita, her ten-year-old granddaughter, was trying to play an anonymous rhapsody whose chords were too spread out for her small hands. Though it was already eleven o'clock in the morning, a lingering chill foreshadowed evening storms. The piano's five-note chant echoed in Nazira's head, but she fancied it was sung by a chorus of voices sent from another world to help her say good-bye to this one. As though suspended in the room's freezing air, the bed seemed to rock to the melody lulling her final moments.

Through the corner of her left eye, Nazira managed to see Angela Tejera's dark visage. Her face full of compassion and her stomach visibly enlarged by pregnancy, the young woman was standing in the doorway, watching her die. She also saw the little table covered with the paraphernalia attending her interminable old age: dark glass bottles, potbellied and svelte, jars of herbal infusions, an old Chinese fan with red flowers painted on a black background, the little bronze bell for calling whoever was in the kitchen, a big bottle of mint and cologne.

Before coming to understand her own death, which attracted her in ways she never could have imagined, she rested her head, still crowned by abundant straw-like hair, on three pillows lightly scented with lavender. She stretched her hand—the right—toward the night stand, and the long fingers covered with translucent skin made a sign in the air, a vague gesture directed toward that lofty and distant heaven high above the moldering ceilings of the house. Angela could not decipher it. Was she seeking redemption? the girl asked herself much later, after the child now enclosed within the egg of her stomach had grown up. Or was she announcing the dawn of a savage era? Was the world of everyday living the sentence no one could escape? she asked herself again, years later, when devout as a novitiate, she bowed before the altar of her enslaved ancestors.

Nazira's hand now rose in the air and stayed there, gesticulating as though its owner were engaged in pleasant conversations with ghosts. And her eyes, those eyes so penetrating they seemed to see and even be in the place where she set about to recapitulate her final days, at the very center of all that tumult.

Suddenly, the faces of her four daughters began to take shape in the room's icy air, superimposing themselves upon the apparitions and circulating through what appeared to be the ancient city of Ur, where miracles surely happened. Her own mother, Rosa Kaltoum, had told her that in the suffocating springtime trees there gave birth to enormous figs, puffed up like black moons, sweet as honeycomb. In Ur, thousands of years ago, merchants transformed garbanzo flour into crimson carpets that took flight with a mere thought or wave of the hand. And crazy mystics fell into trances so they could hear the voices of remote beings.

Long before the daring ones made any discoveries, the people of Ur knew the Earth was a slightly flattened sphere that spun around a ubiquitous star for no reason at all. Long before American jungles were transformed into myths for exhausted civilizations, the people of Ur knew of their existence, innocent and brutal, waiting across the ocean for the downfall of the just. And centuries before astronomers auscultated the heartbeat of the cosmos, caravans of five and six thousand camels started out from Ur and explored the ominous deserts leading to the China Sea.

Nazira contemplated the faces of her four daughters engraved on the grand staircases of the city of Ur. Each of the figures seemed to illustrate a personal destiny devoid of any ancestral traces, and though free of such marks, each one nonetheless condemned to a distinct class of misery brought on by the wretchedness of the times. Widowhood, spinsterhood, onerous conjugal ties, alienation—all could be divined in their portraits.

First, Jasibe's bloated cheeks and the resigned expression she wore for fifty years as she watched Jeremías Berro undress and stretch himself out to snore. Next, Lidia's eyes. Sunken in their sockets, they spoke of her premature widowhood and the exhausting years dedicated to raising Alcira. And then there was Camila's slight retardation. It softened her features, except for the eyes—miles away—which situated her in some unknown place. Finally, Esterina, who became more beautiful with the passing years. Nonetheless, it was impossible to hide her now lascivious mouth, the corners scarred into a grimace of humiliation.

Suddenly Nazira saw herself in an ancient kitchen of Ur. An unexpected flavor coalesces in the orange syrup of apricots. Sweet at first, bitter afterwards, it dates back to the fantastic gardens of the world's infancy. Boiling amber crackles over the flame like a formless mollusk, emitting the glow of sugary vapors. This flavor originated in Ur, in forbidden gardens at first, where, untouched, enormous fruits ripened to magnificence. Now, thousands of years later, with the garden laid to waste by the expulsion of all of humanity, rustling leaves and branches were the only ones left to utter secret tales of sin.

Nazira had nearly completed the dish and was arranging candied apricots, already cold and sculpted in their own syrup, on an iridescent ceramic platter, alternating them with chopped basil. In the middle she placed four figs, one for each of her daughters. There was something shameless about their outsides, a suggestion of indecency within. Exposed by a bite, the interior, with its abundant saliva and spongy hair, mimicked the aroused organs of a carnivorous plant. Submerge them in heavy red wine and let them drown for a night, just as they used to do in Ur, where Nazira now surprisingly found herself, before dying.

She left the kitchen and walked toward the sitting room, down long corridors with sagging ceilings. A strange woman was reclining on a thick rug decorated with arabesques in the conjugal chamber of Ur's royal palace. Soft pillows supported her back. She had been brought there along with other women purchased for the pleasure and relaxation of soldiers returning from a bloody expedition in barbarian lands where men of other tongues and other customs worshipped dark, dreadful gods.

"Tell me a story," Nazira asked the woman without really knowing why. "One of those you tell so well," she asked again, and sat down on the carpet as though surrendering to a kind of comfort she had never known before. The woman's iridescent eyes constantly changed color and her endless, glossy hair was woven into wide nets.

"Ah, yes," she replied. Her voice resonated strangely throughout the palace chamber, echoing over and over again. "The story is the same as always; you already know it. Once, in a faraway place beneath a sulfurous orange sky there was a savage world, populated by reptiles. It was the beginning of time. You know, it's always the beginning. More than life, the Nameless One sought justice, that hidden balance of form and content. And so He urged one of his creatures to transform itself—I don't know if you understand me—to abandon its vile form, its bloody entrails, and become human. Millennia passed. I tell you, thousands of years. The seas rose and fell and rose again. The land froze, thawed, and froze again. The ice heated up, and, liquefied, it flowed downward from melted peaks. Everything was in a state of transformation as it is now."

Nazira listened attentively. It seemed as though she had never heard this incredible story before. She stared closely as the woman's eyes suddenly became two luminous caverns, beckoning with strange sophistry. Enveloped in the woman's voice, Nazira moved closer to her hollow pupils, now two deep tunnels, advancing to swallow her up.

"In a far-off village," the woman managed to say, "there was a girl much like the one you came to be, who cooked apricots in syrup and glazed them with jelly. That exquisite flavor turned any man who tasted it into a righteous person, and although the effect was fleeting, justice was so essential the precarious hero would immediately try to make the world better for everyone."

Nazira traversed the woman's phosphorescent eyes and discovered luminous stretches of the tunnel. Branches of unfamiliar gray bushes and peculiar flowers whose living petals were covered with eyes, with pupils, swayed in front of her. Strange bats hung upside down, asleep, their bodies petrified—not bird-like—but black hearts. She walked slowly, with difficulty, and her ancient silhouette fulfilled a nocturnal desire: to find out what it had all meant, all that weariness, the arduous course of trivial events, the infinitesimal calculus of afternoons and mornings. Now the tunnel curved in on itself in parallel meanderings superimposed one upon the other, like an ocean conch shell leading Nazira ever closer to its center.

❊ *three* ❊

FOR THIRTEEN YEARS Jeremías Berro passed in front of don Alegre Carmona's store and turned his face away, as if to show that he was unaware of the fabric shop's existence. Unaware of its windows covered with petrified dust. Unaware of the presence of don Alegre himself, who, at the very same hour, always stationed himself in the doorway crammed with dangling silken cords and bolts of cloth, for the sole purpose of seeing Jeremías Berro turn his face and continue on his way.

"He can go to hell," don Alegre invariably said to his subordinate, a small, feeble-looking man whose hunched back, sheathed in a gray duster, stood out against the greenish neon light of a clear sky. For a moment the shop assistant's bulging eyes rested on don Alegre's bitter face and his arms hovered halfway between the oak shelving and a wooden ladder propped awkwardly against piles of cloth.

Then he stroked his helmet of dull, nondescript hair and said (as though talking to himself), "It's not g-g-g-ood to hate like that. Around here they s-s-say hat-t-tred twists the m-m-mind and sickens the bod-d-dy."

"Not only should you mind your own business, Beto," don Alegre responded, "but you should also listen to the dictates of the Almighty. It is written that such a swindler—may my tongue fall out at the mention of his name—such a womanizer and public disgrace, shouldn't breathe the same air as me. He shouldn't even live in the same world."

"If you say so, don Alegre. I guess that's how things are," the clerk replied and went back to moving rolls of cloth, comforted by a routine to which there was no possible alternative.

In the meantime, Jeremías Berro had already turned the corner at Pérez Castellano Street—he followed this route purely to irritate Carmona, who always watched him turn his face away—and was traveling down Colón with a half-smile raising the left side of his mouth, though it was hardly noticeable beneath the heavy spiraled mustache covering his thick lips.

He was thinking of Angela Tejera, the black maid his elderly mother-in-law had recently installed in the house. A young thing, but round and robust, her large breasts announced nourishment, mobility. And they would be his to sample just as soon as his mother-in-law finally stopped watching over her so carefully, he told himself. The smile tugged at his mouth again, this time in front of his own store's metal curtain, gleaming calmly in the February morning light. He paused to rummage through the pockets of a vest that strained to cover his protruding, ever-expanding stomach. A watch chain slid through his fat fingers. Eleven fifteen: he was the last one on the block to open up. By now, the others had been inside their places for hours, bustling from cellar to street, writing up orders and C.O.D.'s, taking inventories.

As though rebelling against their fervent work ethic, Jeremías Berro very slowly extracted the curtain's large, heavy key. Indifferently, he put it in the lock, turned it, and then hastily pushed up the grooved iron to reveal a wooden door. He had only to twist the knob slightly and his long narrow salon would come into view.

And just like every other morning, upon entering, he experienced the feeling that this was his true space. Much more than his house and the quarters he shared with Jasibe, it was this room with its checkered floor and strong damp smell that felt most like home.

IT WASN'T THAT Jeremías Berro's daily stroll along the sidewalk in front of his store always gave him heartburn; but rather that, on the contrary, don Alegre Carmona actually required this show of disdain in order to resume an ongoing conversation with the Almighty, one he had initiated more than five years earlier.

As soon as Berro was out of sight, don Alegre would go off to a small room at the rear of the premises, a space that in other times had been used to store remnants and rejects but now held only a small, low, wooden bench where the shopkeeper sat with his face in his hands, firing off challenges to the Almighty.

On this particular morning he complained in a loud voice: "It seems as though wickedness has gone unpunished since the beginning of time. Dear Lord in Heaven, how is it possible? How can it be explained? Or don't I deserve an explanation? Or, at the very least, some kind of understanding? Right here you have the evil example of Jeremías Berro. How come ever since the day he cheated me out of dye imports he's been so happy and successful," finished Carmona just before adding underneath his breath, "and I've been so unfortunate and miserable?"

"You should a-a-add the r-r-rest, don Alegre. Everything that wr-wr-wretch did to his wife and her sisters, not to m-m-mention what they s-s-say he c-c-committed with his niece. Or did you forg-g-get already?" came the clerk's muffled voice from the main room.

Don Alegre let out a curse and quickly prayed that the Almighty hadn't heard. He didn't like being interrupted during his prayers, and liked even less being reminded of the magnitude of Jeremías Berro's sins.

"Didn't I just finish telling you to mind your own business?" grumbled don Alegre. Then he started reciting prayers at the top of his lungs and in Hebrew so the assistant would lose interest in his conversation with the Almighty, an exchange that should be intimate.

To avoid further discussion, Beto turned on the radio. Hadn't his elderly aunt warned him that don Alegre Carmona was going crazy and talking nonsense? Hadn't she warned against wasting time discussing things with him? On the other hand, what could someone like him know about don Alegre's Almighty? Could he by any chance hear voices? His voice? Even the slightest murmur? No. As the years went by, Beto convinced himself that the Almighty spoke only for some people. And even though don Alegre was inspired by a certain piety, nothing could be done to save him from madness. If he couldn't help himself—that growth on his back, the slightly deformed and ill-favored face—he could do even less for Carmona. Let don Alegre commune with phantoms. After all was said and done, a solitary old man, widowed for years and childless, he could afford to fritter away his time, day after day, buried in that storeroom, parked on a stool, talking to the white-washed walls. Let the wandering spirits answer back, not Beto, who usually sat behind the merchandise in the shop window and scrutinized the flow of people passing by, his only intention being to demonstrate his own meekness.

Meanwhile, in the back room, an austere-looking don Alegre Carmona lifted his arms to the ceiling's vague maps of brownish moisture. "This is worse than a vale of tears," he thought. "It's a valley of dark, murky waters." Then he corrected himself, "Better yet, it's a bottomless swamp. And we can always sink a little faster and a little deeper."

Strange images often seemed to materialize on the bare wall, as though his own mind were bringing them before his eyes for no reason. His grandfather Fishel appeared there in a shimmering tunic, and with crook in hand, resolutely ascended a steep stone mountain in Galilee, followed by a community of shepherds. Their flock's prolonged bleating was reminiscent of a lament, a psalmody, something almost human that accompanied the group's pilgrimage upward. No one knew what they would find there at the peak, but they hoped to see the face of God.

Don Alegre Carmona closed his eyes: sometimes they got on his nerves. He wanted to rip them out and humiliate the blackened sockets. Tame them. One shouldn't look at that which wasn't meant to be seen. But in the unreasoning void, his old grandfather Fishel kept on climbing a damned mountain—a steep ascent along a treacherous path where every footfall caused the stones to tremble. Precarious equilibrium. He saw how their sharp edges slashed the souls of his feet. And the leather-like skin that toughened his step. He saw an ancient valley in which a succession of twenty wars had taken place. The parched sand had already swallowed a sea of blood and yet it was once again burdened with dryness.

He'd rip out his brain if that would stop the visions. Scourge his body and his mind. "Come on," he told himself, "You still have two more decades to live."

❊ *four* ❊

THOUGH IGNORANT of her own age and other personal details, Nazira zealously kept track of all the particulars relating to her own discovery of America. Surprisingly, it was Esterina Mualdeb, the one daughter they never expected to amount to much, who sent for her parents and sisters during the uncertain years of the 1920s. The future looked ominous and memories of the past were too fragmented to produce a coherent history, so it seemed like a good time to leave. No one asked how Esterina had scraped together so much money— even in third class, what's known as "steerage," Nazira Mualdeb and José Sus felt rich and pictured their eldest child rolling in New World abundance—how she had managed the impossible task of securing tickets and visas in only four months.

And yet there they were, crammed into the hold of the *Atlantic Pearl*, dazed by the glare of an ocean so huge and flat it seemed like a brutal, motionless desert.

"The Earth is round," José Sus told Nazira, in an attempt to comfort her just before they embarked, "so we won't fall into the abyss. And don't worry about the girls either." Nazira took a few moments to think about her husband's words. They simply confirmed the rumors she had heard from people who knew how to read newspapers and books. A torrent of resourcefulness settled into her heart: life was smoothing the way for her and she was gliding along the surface of a sphere hurled into the void, a sphere on which every path led back to the beginning. From then on she would never be afraid again.

The Uruguayan consulate in Aleppo consisted of a lone bureaucrat who came from Rome once a year to grant temporary residence permits. He embossed his official seal on hieratic photographs that captured the way they looked at the moment—portraits they would soon cease to resemble. "You want to travel to America? To the Republic of Uruguay?" the incredulous official repeatedly asked in a shaky mixture of Italian and Arabic. As he spoke, his eyes took in the line of poor unfortunates waiting their turn to go anywhere. "You and your four daughters?" the man asked again. José Sus took great satisfaction in setting him straight. "No. There are only three daughters. The oldest has already settled there. And she's meeting us."

"Are you sure you want to go to Uruguay?" the man asked once more, or maybe it was his duty to ask and thus prevent possible suicides on the open sea. He pulled a dog-eared pamphlet from his drawer, its cover displaying a narrow street in a city that was less than resplendent. There were rows of cable cars and three or four automobiles (one an open convertible) with huge headlights passing through an odd assortment of pedestrians who crossed the pavement in every direction. The men wore solemn-looking hats and grave, preoccupied expressions. The women had on strange head gear pulled all the way down to their eyes, long narrow skirts, and fur stoles.

"This is Montevideo," said the official. "The main street," he added as he got ready to put the file away. But José Sus held on to it. He took out a pair of pince-nez attached to a heavy black cord and slipped them over his protruding nose. He was a slightly built man, much shorter than his spouse. Seeing them together, the functionary conceptualized husband and wife as a single being, compound and complementary, there to have him decide its destiny. José Sus saw the silhouettes of tall buildings with overhanging marble balconies. And decorative stained glass. Rather ostentatious facades, from what he knew of architecture. He saw figures wrapped in long winter overcoats. On the next page a pair of dancers assumed a strangely contorted pose: the man, in a wide-brimmed hat, striped pants, and cape, was bending a woman over his left knee. Wearing a slit skirt that exposed most of her thigh, she shamelessly sat on his leg. What was going on at the far ends of the earth? José Sus wondered.

The functionary, now indifferent, showed him one more example. "It's soccer," he said, "the most popular sport in Uruguay." José Sus felt ashamed of his coarse tinsmith's hands and turned another page. There he saw three individuals in dark knee-length undershorts and long white socks. They were engrossed in what seemed to be a furious battle, pointing their toes at a ball that had escaped to the lower right-hand corner of the photograph. The background was made up of a huge playing field filled with flags and people. "I never owned a ball," said José Sus as he softly closed the booklet. But the official had already lowered his gaze to fill out the proper forms.

While automatically answering his questions, Nazira Mualdeb thought about the bundles of cotton sheets she needed to bring along, about the tablecloths hand-embroidered by her own mother. They were already terribly old but would nonetheless cross the sea as neither her mother, nor her mother's mother ever had. Landlocked, wandering old gypsies, tablecloth embroiderers—their rags had outlived them and would soon see that blessed place where her daughter and granddaughter ate in dignified peace on every one of the Lord's holy days.

✽ five ✽

THE PERFUME BUSINESS wasn't for just anyone. It took special skill to stock shop windows with vials, bottles, and huge greenish flasks full of macerated essences that shimmered mysteriously as they gave birth to unparalleled aromas. Jeremías Berro had inherited the archaic knowledge through his umbilical cord and it could be summed up in one simple phrase: "business is an art, and a perfume business is the most sublime art of all." So there could be no doubt on the subject, the words *Perfumes of Carthage* were painted in deep violet over his doorway. Jeremías Berro had often observed the way ladies reacted to this intense hue and he could vouch for its positive effect on business. Beneath the letters stood a display case that had once been a stained-glass window but now exhibited forty receptacles of every shape and color containing distilled, acidified, and fermented concoctions overheating in the morning sun.

By contrast, the interior was dark and in many ways looked like a greenhouse where wide beds of rare plants could fulfill their destinies in the shadows. Stills, test tubes, and glass bulbs resting on extinguished gas burners turned the back room into a kind of primitive laboratory for impromptu experimentation. *Perfumes of Carthage* wasn't just a name meant to evoke fragments of lost worlds for frenzied people bathed in stale Montevidean sweat. Jeremías Berro wanted more than that. He wanted to invite his customers to dream of distant places, long-extinct crossroads where refined faces and smooth bodies experienced rare, ephemeral joys. For him, Carthage suggested the convergence of pleasure and heroism in their most sensual extremes: Hannibal and his fleet entering vanquished Greek cities on a calm Mediterranean afternoon more than two thousand years ago, and the insistent fragrance of olive trees flourishing at the edge of the sea. Because in the present, life just slipped away, lost to a sober upbringing, work, and a predetermined future. Hardly reasonable. Deadened senses, thought Jeremías Berro, in a deadened land where European brutalities arrived without fanfare.

Once again, he thought about Angela Tejera's breasts, and something began to happen beneath his bulging stomach. Vertiginous desire sparked the imaginary lines of an epic poem in which he described her breasts as she herself would never see them. He dreamed of running toward the house on Ituzaingó street, slipping undetected into the attic room and under his mother-in-law's bed—there to hide and, hopefully, watch Angela use the chamber pot in the middle of the night. To hear the tinkling of the liquid, its aroma touched with sandalwood and acacia—perhaps a bit more robust— and wait. Then, all of a sudden, from below the bed, he'd grab her by the ankles—force her to stay crouched down on her haunches— and moving the receptacle aside, slip his erect tongue into the musky flavors of her dark vulva, there to probe the origin of his improper passion.

Something distracted him from his reverie. There was a growing hubbub in the street, punctuated by three short, dry explosions, breaking glass, and panicked footsteps. Jeremías looked up and saw the backs of two individuals hiding in his shop's vestibule. Pressed up against the wall, they inched away from the sidewalk without turning around. Outside, people were shouting and slamming their doors and windows.

Jeremías Berro moved out from behind his work table and opened the glass door. "Come in," he whispered cautiously. Still huddled against the wall, the pair turned their frightened faces. They looked stunned, as though they hadn't expected to see anyone. "Get moving," Jeremías repeated as he held the door open for them. With a sigh of relief, they entered the store, which seemed tranquil and sleepy compared to the street.

"Thank you, señor, thank you very much," one of them gasped, recovering his voice. They were young—no more than twenty years old—disheveled, and sweaty; yet one could still see the trace of distinguished origins in their appearance.

"I'm Anselmo Tartaglia," said the first speaker by way of introduction. "And this is my brother, Gualberto." He finished with a vague reference: "We come from Rio Negro. You know what I mean."

Jeremías had no idea what they were talking about, but he offered the two young men some of the café Moka he was simmering on the gas burner. The one called Gualberto asked what it was since they had never seen such a thick, black brew. "Turkish coffee," explained Jeremías Berro, and he gave them a brief history of his arrival at the port of Montevideo several years back. The young men looked at one another.

"So you don't know what's happening out there," said Anselmo. "They certainly don't explain the current situation to Gringos," added Gualberto.

Anselmo spoke again: "Whether or not you believe it, señor, we're in the middle of a revolution," and he started to tell Jeremías a fascinating story. In case he didn't know it yet, this country, which attracted so many of his kind, was living under a dictatorship. That meant the government hadn't been chosen by democratic means. Instead, persecution and fraud took priority over constitutional law. Did Jeremías understand? And although that government was almost two years old and demanded everyone's support, it had failed to prove its legitimacy to true patriots, men of good will who had sworn a mutual pact of honor to overthrow it. Now did Jeremías understand what was happening?

"Yes," said Jeremías, and then he asked where those men were. "In Paso Morlán, on the banks of the Colla river," said Gualberto. "In Soriano, in Cerro Chato, in San Ramón, in Tupambaé," said Anselmo. And they described the confrontation with government troops, in their eyes a modest first victory auguring future successes. They explained that they had come from the rebel camp itself because their father wanted to keep them out of new skirmishes with the army. But they weren't children, and as soon as they arrived in Montevideo, they had taken to the streets with signs and posters, hoping to rally support and tell the people of the south what was going on up north.

After listening attentively, Jeremías Berro asked what ideas the patriots espoused. "There are possibilists from the *Blanco* party and democrats from the *Colorados,*" the young men answered in unison. "Not to mention anarchists, socialists, and all kinds of dreamers," they added. "What unites us is the desire for a free country and a legitimate government," they finally smiled, empty coffee cups in hand.

"Good," said Jeremías Berro, "just what I've been looking for. I want the same things for this country, since it's mine now. I want to join you."

❊ *six* ❊

THE LAWYER WAS NATIVE BORN—about thirty years old—wearing a dark suit and stiff collar and he smiled at her as he nodded his head. Holding Lunita in her arms, Esterina Mualdeb finally sat down and let a deep sigh escape from her troubled breast. "This is a divorce agreement," she heard him explain, "and it's completely valid."

Esterina mustered the energy to ask how it could be valid if she had never put her signature on anything, if she had systematically refused to sign the paper each time her husband beat her and locked her up. "But that's precisely the point," smiled the attorney. "There's an X here and the witnesses state that you don't know how to sign your name." With Lunita clinging to her body like a frightened animal, Esterina buried her chin in the child's curls. The lawyer cleared his throat when he saw tears trembling in the eyes of this desperate young woman who had carried her little girl up three flights of stairs to reach his office on Piedras Street. Then he rose from his swivel chair, walked around the enormous rectangle of a desk, and edged toward her.

Placing his hand on the silk strap of the dress she herself had sewn for solemn occasions, he whispered into Esterina's ear, "Come, now, don't be so upset." He found her disturbingly beautiful—even though she was crying and holding a two-year-old in her arms—and slid his hand toward her neck, where a heavy black chignon threatened to tumble out of its net and come undone. She lifted her surprised face. The lawyer's eyes were propositioning her. If she was willing, he would do everything possible.. . .

Esterina quickly rose to her feet. Alarmed, the man stepped away. She choked back her bitterness, lowered her eyes, and bounded out of the room without looking at him. It was true that she didn't know how to write—how could a mere seamstress from Aleppo's Jewish quarter, a girl who hadn't been allowed to go to school, know anything? But what kind of strange country was this where things got done in exchange for personal favors?

Once out on the street, she walked and walked, without knowing where she was headed. The weight of the little girl, passive and still in her arms, served as both a comfort and an incentive. Bit by bit her feelings of impotence and anguish turned to rancor, a harsh, biting rancor that she carried with her as she ascended the steps leading to don Zaquím Salam, translator of thirty-four languages and an old compatriot of her father's back in Syria.

Zaquím Salam peeked out onto the landing when he heard Esterina's footsteps, each one more weary than the last as she climbed up four flights of stairs. He asked her to sit in the little waiting room and then withdrew behind the opaline glass of his office door.

She placed the now-sleeping child on her lap and with a handkerchief embroidered in violet thread, dried the perspiration from her cleavage. It was the middle of a February that simply wouldn't cool off. Don Zaquím came to the door to say good-bye to a small, dark fig of an old man. Then with a sweep of his arm, he invited her to come in.

Handing him the paper she had retrieved from the lawyer and foregoing the usual half hour of courtesies, Esterina nervously blurted out: "Here, don Zaquím, I brought you this. I want your advice." Her voice broke on the final word.

Don Zaquím Salam was a corpulent man whose full, dark face boasted an enormous hooked nose and fleshy lips just barely covered by a luxuriant mustache that curled up at the ends. Abundant gray hair formed a wavy helmet over his skull.

"We know about your case," he admitted condescendingly as he set the document aside. "Your husband has been all over Montevideo, showing off a sedan fully equipped with every housemaid who happens to cross in its path. Let's be honest. America hasn't done you much good. That whole business about the deportation order for you and your daughter was a disgrace. I'm just glad they canceled it in time. As for your being left out on the street, there's certainly no remedy for that and, I must say, it does reflect badly on one of our own. If I didn't have so much respect for that bum's late grandfather, God rest his soul, you can imagine what I'd do to him," said don Zaquím with a concerned face.

Esterina felt comforted by his words. She needed to hear them from someone. In that motherless and fatherless foreign land, don Zaquím sounded just like José Sus, her own father, who most certainly would have left his home and crossed the sea to defend his stricken daughter from the abuses of such a wicked husband.

"*Alah mácon*, may good fortune be with you," said Zaquím as though interpreting her very thoughts, and he flashed a smile full of big, wide, yellow teeth. It helped to assuage some of the grief and left Esterina feeling almost free to accept her own desolation, her undeserved poverty, and that share of stupidity we all carry around with us.

"On the other hand, my child," continued Zaquím, "why shouldn't you have a great future? In Aramaic we say *m'zal*; in Hebrew, *mazal*. Luck, young lady. Your name is derived from the Sumerian. Ishtar. That says it all. You represent the goddess of love who dwelled on Venus, so I have something very special for you," he explained and then, in a Spanish replete with reversed p's and b's, told her about a woman he knew—respectable, very attractive—who ran a boardinghouse on Cerrito Street. Girls and women (either single or separated) gathered there to dance and sing with respectable gentlemen who were seeking a healthy diversion to relieve boredom and fill the empty hours. Nothing indecent, mind you. Lots of young women from Poland and Lithuania, though the most sought-after beauties were like her, Syrians who spoke French or French girls with Syrian parents. "All of them, our kind," don Zaquím added enthusiastically. And if she said yes, if she really wanted to get ahead, he saw nothing wrong with it.

Esterina instinctively recoiled and embraced her sleeping child. But don Zaquím was already enumerating the attractive details of her new life: she would have a room for herself and the little girl, and meals, and the chance to send for her parents and sisters. Working only at night, she would even be able to recover her health and perhaps, in time, buy a sewing machine (on credit—for a future dressmaker's shop) like the one she had left, at great personal sacrifice, back in Aleppo. Yes, there was no doubt about it, life was smiling at her again and opportunity was knocking at the door.

Somewhat faint, Esterina descended the long marble staircase, leaning on the railing for support and holding Luniţa against her left shoulder, afraid the mixture of dizziness and joy would split her head open.

✾ *ʃeven* ✾

AFTER SIX WEEKS of restless waves, José Sus had a clear impression of the sea: it involved the waters of an ancient flood, still-turbulent waters bearing memories of the first global destruction. Like an ark attempting to save a basic remnant of humanity with one grand, final gesture, the ship traveled through this vast expanse with three hundred pilgrims crowded together on the floor of the hold in third class. They'd been swallowed by a strange Leviathan and were being macerated in its stomach—having said good-bye forever to the lands of their parents, if not of their grandparents, who were also gypsies—primed for the next inferno arriving from the southwest.

The horizon stayed fixed for days, and to José Sus it seemed as though they were suspended in a void, without time, without old age. Crouched on deck, inhaling scented tobacco through his bronze *narguile*, he imagined Uruguay as a jungle where small agile monkeys scampered down mottled coconut palms. In the distance, he could almost see naked innocents tending small gardens full of watermelons as big as houses and tomatoes ready to burst through their skins. It would be a land knowing neither hatred nor stigma. A land without evil. There beneath a blazing sun, his white skin would acquire an Adamic hue. And beneath a compassionate breeze, he would find respite from the inheritance of ancient sorrows embedded in his very being.

Then, the ship seemed to resume course, creating two white trails in its wake and the weightless sensation that only occurs when one is afloat. Long days sailing toward a melancholy promised land. It felt as though nothing had happened between the journey of Abram Neftali Sus, his great, great-grandfather who had fled the Kingdom of Leon a little more than four centuries earlier, and this journey of his. Wasn't it the same sea? The same waves? And couldn't you swear it was even the same unfathomable immensity? Lost in thought, in a permanent daydream, José Sus had no idea whether he was awake or asleep. He ate sparingly, as though his body had disappeared, and a worried Nazira plied with him with dried figs, toasted pumpkin seeds, and carefully peeled pistachios.

"Could he be ill?" she asked, searching her husband's face. "Could he be homesick?" she loudly inquired of no one in particular.

"I'll never set foot in the new land. I'll only be allowed to contemplate it from afar, as the patriarch did in Canaan," answered José Sus and then he returned to his dream state.

"God forgive you for saying such a thing," Nazira replied, but the roar of the sea drowned out her words.

José Sus saw naked women with wind-swept hair riding chargers across the water. They flashed in front of him and disappeared instantly, swallowed by an infernal monster from the murky depths who reared a flat, saurian, troglodyte head covered with seaweed hair. José Sus saw trapezoidal sails with equilateral crosses searching for a fugitive wind. Then ancient schooners, ghostly frigates, sketched in by the dawn mist. All of them deserted, their wheels adrift on the bridges, like sarcophagi floating toward other worlds. Sometimes he saw fire on the water, flames from the distant past, and he even heard the cries of sailors dragged down by the abyssal currents: the ocean was bringing forth the specters of all its battles.

There was something familiar in the hum of that monumental stew's incessant complaint. It beckoned him. At midnight, choruses of sopranos appeared out of nowhere to parody religious psalms. Voracious medusas took shape in the keel and multiform hydras laid siege to portholes, rendering them impassable.

Someone mentioned sirens who would rise to the surface—their macabre tresses flowing like live eels—and beg men to free them from a dark fate.

There was talk of submerged cemeteries prowling beneath the ships, waiting to capsize them. Promontories of human bones roaming endlessly to and fro, spinning and whirling like grotesque helices. José Sus understood that the sea was older than the land, that it flowed into every hollow of the earth and patiently wore away the sharp edges of the stones.

One day someone said, "Come on now, wake up. We're arriving at port."

José Sus opened his eyes and saw a hill slipping by to the left, surrounded by a valley of tiny provincial houses. Puffs of black breath spilled from the port's deep cleft where tall, slender masts, superimposed one upon the other, formed delicate, lacy designs. The ocean contracted in spite of itself, giving birth to a calm, coppery river that penetrated the landscape and rose up toward a bend.

José Sus watched as Nazira suddenly appeared and opened her slender arms to embrace the coastline. They looked at one another and cried. The girls, a bit farther away, remained unmoved as they tucked their braids into scarves firmly knotted at the chin. Red fishing boats overflowing with dead catch allowed themselves to be rocked by the muddy domestic waters. An old fisherman, naked from the waist up, waved his anonymous welcome from one of them.

Later everything was euphoria, expectation, and confusion. Especially when they were told that José Sus had not come down yet. And when they finally found him—gone—felled by some antiquated fishing tackle that had sprung up from nowhere. His heart was no longer beating but his face retained a look of reverie.

❊ *eight* ❊

JEREMÍAS BERRO'S ONGOING INFIDELITIES with a succession of household servants were public knowledge. Though women of the neighborhood maliciously called him "perfumer to wives and bedrooms," local gossip was just too weak an antidote to cure him of his philandering ways. The luxuriant spiral mustache and full cheeks gave his rosy paternal face a playful, inviting air, making him irresistible to ladies of all ages. His wife Jasibe accused him of being entirely too friendly with everyone—including herself—and she took shelter in her dressing room, fleeing from Jeremías's slimy grasp as though it were the plague. Once safely locked inside, she could contemplate the whiteness of her soft, plump body and take pride in the fact that she never allowed her husband to do the same.

He fell on top of her every Saturday night, not caring whose arms had held him in the afternoon. But Jasibe defended herself with layers of sheets secured by bows and lacing, so her husband was left to charge against a shadowy cavern, without ever managing to temper his wife's body as had always been expected of men throughout ages and ages of unbridled copulation.

That is how Jasibe was able to preserve a certain cleanliness—if not purity—in the midst of so much excess. What was lust if not this? Her husband forcing his breath on anyone at hand. Angela Tejera would be no exception. Hers was the familiar story of a child conceived by mistake, without a father to give her a name or food for a swollen belly—a man already worn out from his other children—in some hick town that probably no longer existed. People like her were forever appearing out of nowhere, toting all their possessions, ready to accept whatever might come their way. And if it turned out to be the house full of extended family where Jeremías Berro lived with his wife, her sisters, his mother-in-law, and the rest of their nieces, nephews, and relatives, not to mention a mysterious tenant, so much the better, since among all those people there would always be someone she could go to for help.

Angela had been assigned to take care of the old woman whose death rattles—night in and night out—had little to do with her final agony. Instead they heralded startling dreams, dreams she used to prolong her remaining years. The very first night, in her poorly spoken Spanish full of b's transformed into p's, Nazira had confessed to the girl that every dream created a small opening through which time breathed a bit more of itself into her life. No one else, Nazira explained, must ever know this secret. Only Angela, because when the end arrived, she would be the one to soothe her in her final moments. The length of one's days, Nazira used to say, actually depended on oneself: if you dreamed fervently, you could cross the threshold and a sudden blast of events would be added to those already granted to you.

Angela listened attentively to these revelations, but found nothing pertinent in them. All of twenty years old, she saw any life over forty as excessive, and so, curled up beneath the old woman's bed, next to the enameled chamber pot where urine was decanted each night, she silently resented Nazira's persistent will to live. Who would want to hang around so long and for what? she asked herself. It wasn't her problem to find the answer, nor to know what to do with each one of those minutes and hours of other people's lives.

She heard poorly disguised footsteps creak softly on the padded wooden stairs that led to the small attic, and she held her breath. Soon, a sliver of light from the hallway split the room's semidarkness, stretching all the way from the dovetailed floorboards to the high sloped ceiling. She could see a man's strong, hairy feet against the light of the half-opened door and two powerful calves rising up to a silk robe. Its crooked hem trembled imperceptibly. Angela hunkered down toward the foot of the old woman's bed. It was the second night she had been terrified to discover Jeremías Berro's two feet standing there in the doorway, his eyes searching myopically for her to move, make some gesture, rise up seminude, black breasts oscillating in the darkness, to go off with him, enslaved like her ancestors, to the inferno of forbidden worlds.

But instead, she hid under her blanket and once again pretended to be asleep, armored by a kind of stillness that brings every intention to a dead stop and leaves each proposition in parentheses. The feet spun hastily about, the door closed, and she heard stairs creaking softly again, burdened by someone's heavy descent to the dining room. A trickle of perspiration cut between Angela's breasts like a hot, oiled blade and sliced a gash next to her pounding heart.

✳ *nine* ✳

BY THE END OF SUMMER, Esterina's life had taken an unusual turn. It began with three meals a day for herself and Lunita, who, thanks to don Zaquím Salam—God bless him and keep him—was growing fat and developing plump, rosy cheeks in doña Regina's care. What is more, Esterina had exchanged the shabby, discreet dresses she carefully preserved throughout five years of marriage, for a new wardrobe consisting of colorful, frivolous things with plunging necklines. There were full skirts in flowery prints for daytime, and for the evening, sleek satin gowns of red or green, cut low to show the neck and expose plenty of cleavage, thus making her bosom seem more ample and compliant.

It would be inappropriate to speak of prostitution, especially since such a term could hardly describe what Esterina thought of her work. As long as Lunita was safe—spending her days with doña Regina and her nights with Clotilde (doña Regina's elderly mother), who brought the little one over to her house for dinner and a good night's sleep—the world wasn't such a thankless place.

Of course, many of the others complained: Polish girls whose passage had been paid by putative fiancés making money hand over fist in a bountiful America. Girls brought in from the now-boarded-up houses on Yerbal Street and already on their second or third illness. Disease-ridden girls who were mired in a kind of decadence that would never see a reprieve from either clients or owners. Girls who had dreamt of becoming vaudeville stars and imagined rising up from their humble origins to encounter that special someone whose mad heroism would save them from a life of perversity. Their curses could be heard in several languages, and in the restless diurnal dreams of women dazed by the routine spilling of *caña dulce* and semen into their guts.

And of course the pay was nearly nonexistent: a few second-hand frocks, some eau de cologne, the occasional wilted bouquet rejected by a girlfriend or wife. And that joke of a lunch, barely digested between cries and unanswered questions. Passports were gone forever and letters home were individually monitored by the wise and practical mind of doña Regina, who didn't hesitate to call on the owners if things became difficult. An occasional thrashing quelled complaints for a while. They would hear muffled blows coming from the room below and bottles smashing against the walls. The weekly balancing of accounts was sacred.

But Esterina came from a husband who locked her up for five days and nights without food in a moldy Spanish-style armoire, while he carried on with the landlady. From a husband who peddled corsets and pin-tucked linens door to door and then at night grabbed her by the hair, threw her down, and fornicated in a rage. After that he made her work at the sewing machine until 6:00 A.M., producing slips and petticoats to be sold during the day. A man who tied her up to the bed hinges before he left, even though it would probably never occur to her to look at anyone else. She was expected to squat down on all fours and wash the baseboards with her tongue.

So, in spite of everything, Esterina saw her job as a form of protection against a marriage made in hell (that is, if one could manage to apply this locution to a world with no escape). Though an uncomplicated perspective, it would require a good dose of resignation. Of course, this house had nothing in common with the ones they had closed over on Yerbal Street. The difference could be seen in a glance (at least in principle). She, like the others, was there to oblige a mature clientele, most of them over forty. Married men or widowers who had achieved a certain level of material well-being (despite the crises of recent years) but who found their homes too serious or solemn for relaxation.

"It's so different here," they used to say. "I feel good here—loved—and I can be myself."

Esterina would agree and give them another serving of *caña* in a small heavy glass. After realizing just what her ex-husband had done to her life, she developed a devout indifference toward men. They were partial beings, incomplete, their constitutions lacking some critical piece. She couldn't say what it was with scientific certainty. Something like a definitive experience that kept them from truly getting to the bottom of things.

Women, on the other hand, all seemed to function on a different level, one distinguished by a kind of daily perseverance that made them somehow more insightful. Each one, in spite of her many sufferings, demonstrated a certain competence, an expertise. Esterina could see through them as though they were transparent.

"How are things at work?" Nazira would ask when her daughter came to visit on Sunday afternoons, pretending to have a job she never talked about in some hat shop in Aguada. "Nothing new," Esterina invariably responded as she assumed her best expression of boredom, all the while afraid her mother might read the lie in that familiar phrase.

But Nazira was aging in a private dream world. Her daughters had become relative strangers, and the only spouse who lived under her roof, that shameless Jeremías Berro, bore no resemblance to a proper Jewish husband from Aleppo. This failure of comprehension kept her from fathoming her child's words. She did indeed note a change, above all in Esterina and Lunita's physical appearance; but in this strange place, good times were decided by chance.

"You seem so much better," her sisters said and drank a toast to her steady job, thanking the good don Zaquím for having found it. With small cups raised to the late afternoon glow of the skylight, they proposed "an anisette to don Zaquím." Even Camila, in recent months more quiet than usual, gave an approving look.

One night, a tall stranger with a serious face—was he ever capable of smiling?—showed up at doña Regina's, barely responding when she asked what he wanted. Esterina never found out why he chose her, shorter and more full bodied than the rest and still looking like someone who had known a more decent kind of life. "A good girl who fell on hard times" is what the others mockingly called her.

There was a kind of restraint in the way he undressed, placing his jacket and pants over the chair with unexpected delicacy. With equal care, he removed a dark, long-barreled revolver from its fraying holster and put it among the atomizers infected with cheap cologne on the night stand. Then he made her sit down on the unmade bed. She was wearing her long black dressing gown decorated with red dragons and it all seemed like business as usual. "Let's at least try to keep up appearances," he explained in a dry voice, "even though I'm not going to touch you. I have three hours to kill before I can hit the road. And this is the safest place. The white guards will never think to look for me here," he chuckled softly, removing a cigarette from a silver-plated case and pensively caressing it with his fingers.

He spoke with enormous reserve, almost through clenched teeth, and she listened to him with a fascination for words that was utterly new to her. Though nearly naked, she felt her body relax while he expressed his hatred of injustice and indifference, and of men who enthroned themselves in their posts while giving in to corruption. He talked about his skepticism: political parties disgusted him. One by one, they were all contaminated by the same kind of incompetent individuals, birds of prey, dedicated to upholding rules and regulations created to protect their own interests.

Around four in the morning, after downing two liters of *caña*, he started hurling accusations and naming names, concluding with a bit of self-reflection, spoken guardedly, almost a confession. "I'm an anarchist," he said. "From Buenos Aires. I crossed the river in a canoe."

Suddenly he was asleep, head on his chest and long mustache touching his collar bone. She covered him with her own blanket and adjusted the pillows. Then she got into bed and, lying next to him, studied his face, until her own eyelids sank heavily into a dreamy abyss.

❧ *ten* ❧

A LONG BELCH that seemed to rise from the depths of a subterranean cavern inaugurated Nazira's naps and, like a household clock, established the afternoon rhythms of a waning summer. The year 1935 had itself begun without any originality: abundant waves of damp heat settled over the patio, misting the opaline skylight. Angela Tejera peeked through the doorway and saw her charge fall asleep to the undulant rhythm of her own breathing.

Light beams pierced the gaps in the attic's worn shutters and illuminated the elderly matriarch's profile. Chiseled by the hand of a fierce God, the bony contours of her face suddenly stood out in high relief, the translucent skin revealing an angular skull and collapsing valleys of wrinkled flesh. Surmising Nazira's age, Angela reminded herself that more than one hundred thirty years anesthetized even the most cataclysmic life, and she wondered how much longer the meticulously braided straw-like hair would flutter on the pillow, how much longer those delicate hands would softly press against the sheet's arabesque.

After breakfast, the smell of sesame-flavored meatballs lingered in the house like an invisible guest and settled over the darkened living room's shabby wicker armchairs. In her dream, Nazira flew over the deep blue Mediterranean Sea and returned to the thronging *Djamiliyeh*, Aleppo's Jewish quarter, built atop countless buried civilizations. Descending in a cloud of smoke, she peered down at the old market where the swarms of people looked like a vital, boiling liquid.

The wind inflated her long skirts and she floated down vertically, feet pressed together, legs stiff as pillars, landing perfectly upright on the slippery stones surrounding a deep well. Copper-colored people in strange headgear flowed past her, talking noisily, shouting in unintelligible languages, and balancing all sorts of objects on their skulls: enormous bundles of linens, bales of brightly dyed cotton fabric, pots of dried fruit, and pitchers of sky blue water warmed by the noonday sun.

She walked toward her lover's house. It was no longer necessary to worry about being seen. The narrow streets rose upward, zigzagging along with the crowds of people. His mosaic vestibule reflected the late morning's azure light and cast a greenish hue over the patio where a small stream wept into a pool—like a fountain. Toufik Ibn Moussa was standing in the doorway to a shadowy bedroom adorned with piles of rugs. Two small watery eyes smiled beneath his bald pate.

With a welcoming sweep of his hand—a gesture that was both sensuous and familiar, exposing a huge belly interrupted by a frieze of downy white hair—he invited Nazira to enter his abode. Now earthbound, she came inside and deposited her shawls, blouses, skirts, and petticoats on the carpet. Then Toufik made a sign and she stretched herself out on the floor, completely nude, backbone flat against the low, uneven coolness of the tiles. The body in her dream was as old as the one taking an afternoon nap in Montevideo's summertime: thin, bony, and over one hundred thirty years old.

"You'll have many children because your abdomen is as soft as the sands of Et Tabun," Toufik said in the guttural tones of his Judeo-Arab dialect, "and it's as slippery as the oil of ripe olives."

Nazira slowly opened her thighs. Toufik placed his ungainly hand over the orifice from which a hot serum flowed and there it remained as he spoke: "You will have four hundred children, but never know most of them. They will scatter throughout the earth, carrying you— your pieces—each one leaving the same mark. You'll see." And he slipped inside of her, staying there for seven hours, holding her curved torso beneath his body while her breasts rose up like the sand dunes of Judea. Aflame, she encircled him with two skeletal femurs, knowing she must already be pregnant, flooded with an exploding interior light that burst through her skin.

Nazira felt as though she had secretly received a magic charm in her advanced old age, a sticky coating of ointment, invisible to her father Shabtay, invisible to mothers and to gods. She saw herself giving birth to four hundred children, one after another, males and females, their small astonished heads emerging from her womb—a human spillway—escaping through a fissure that hurled them into life. One by one the tiny, purple, scab-encrusted bodies weighed anchor and broke free, thrown into the void, the throng of humanity, the bitter upheaval.

On his side with his back to her, Toufik was already launching snores and spurious exhalations into the atmosphere. He dreamed a dream of sea voyages, of sailing vessels crossing an ancient Mediterranean dawn before the advent of writing. Horizons were broader back then and the smell of dun-colored ocean eels rose toward the long oars only to be swallowed up by a resounding chorus of Nubian slaves swaying in unison throughout the length of the ship.

Curled up behind the ladder to the hold, he could see a passing snippet of sky, its quota of stars dimmed by the rising sun. He was a sickly boy of thirteen. After many years, his parents had finally secured the silks and dyestuffs necessary to bribe a trafficker who rented boats from the Carthaginian fleet and used them to deliver slaves bought and sold in Alexandria. So in the company of black kings with impenetrable faces, women moaning in various languages, and babies fatally torn from their mothers' breasts, Toufik traveled to Alexandria, the marvelous.

During the day, he was tormented by the murmuring of people resigned to an ill-starred fate. At night—their forms now hieratic and their tears exhausted—they looked like stone statues beneath the sky's impassive moon. Arrival at port was announced by the raising of sails and that singular stampede of passengers with baggage and wild schemes. By dwarves who danced and told fortunes, newly arrived from remote villages. And by that sense of foreignness he so adored in his yearning to experience the rare and the incredible, far from the ironmonger's shop where sparks singed his father's pupils, far from Bahasita, as the Jewish quarter was known to its inhabitants back in Aleppo.

For a while he stayed with his aunt and uncle, the Adisis, in the Jewish district near Necropolis, where dyers from Brindisi, tanners from Constantinople, and glass-blowers from Venice all converged to trade their spices, jade, and bales of cotton.

Now he saw the tower of Lighthouse Island, like a second sun burning in the dawn. And the palaces and temples climbing up from port toward the hills, their marble terraces dyed the color of rosy Passover wine. Near the wharves, the hubbub had already engulfed an early market where strangers, soldiers, and whores acted out tales of joy and tragedy. The world was once a deafening maelstrom, Toufik remembered, more amazing by the minute.

eleven

SHE MET HER FIRST FLAME at Club Lezama. A jet black girl from Pando—a laundress who had already experienced a bit of life—brought her to the dance. Angela was wearing a shiny silk hand-me-down dress. Someone mentioned that it had quite a history. Nazira's father bought the gown back in old Damascus so she could wear it to meet the family of a potential husband with whom they were about to arrange a fitting and proper marriage. Unfortunately, the deal fell through when they discovered the young candidate was nicknamed Nuri, just like his future father-in-law, who instantly panicked and broke off the proposed engagement. He was afraid of demons. It was a sign of unequivocal bad luck to have the same name as one's son-in-law: as soon as the marriage was consummated, a terrible disaster would befall the wife's father, something like a grave illness or even death itself. Why take risks when there were plenty of other men with different names to marry his daughters.

Nevertheless, even now, if held up to the light, the bodice showed faint round water stains; because Nazira had wept bitter tears over the ridiculous prohibition that barred her from marrying someone she had glimpsed in dreams and through half-closed shutters, someone who touched her with unexpected emotion. Still and all, the dress was brought to Montevideo and passed down to Jasibe, until obesity and matronly inertia prevented her from squeezing into it. Then Lidia inherited the family treasure, even though the silk looked like a graceless curtain on her scrawny, flat-chested body. Many other garments could claim similar genealogical histories, bequests connecting mothers, daughters, and grandmothers in a repetition of ancient images. But this dress had witnessed drastic circumstances, refusing seduction and fading ever so slightly despite the tender care of those who lacked the acquisitive power to abandon the old.

So, steeped in ancient perfumes—a blend of violets and stale perspiration held in check by modesty—the dress ended up on Angela Tejera's mulatto body the night of the New Year's Eve gala at the end of 1934. No outfit seemed to stand out in the crowd at Club Lezama in Aguada that evening because the enormous dance floor was packed with people waiting for the orchestra to begin. When the musicians finally took the stage, still more customers left the tables surrounded by stretches of immense windows and pushed their way onto the floor, ready for the downbeat. They were either established couples or recently introduced strangers setting forth on the ritualized odyssey of getting acquainted.

Angela watched Demetria disappear, pulled away by a swarthy fellow with extravagant hair and a narrow gaze who nodded at them and introduced himself as having come from Rivera to celebrate the New Year. She was left alone among all those people, not knowing what to do with her arms or the small shiny purse suspended from them. Her face felt damp and the hair that had been so patiently smoothed out with Vaseline and tucked beneath Nazira's little black hat escaped from its careful chignon and sprouted rebellious spiraling curls. She felt very black among all those white people. Looking at her own dun-colored arms, she wondered why she had come. "Don't worry so much about skin color," insisted Demetria. "Men are curious about *mulattas*. And since this dance is for everyone, you belong here too."

And although Demetria's argument sounded reasonable to Angela, in practice, she couldn't help feeling a certain inadequacy: standing there, in the middle of a dance for white people, most of them laborers, or employees of workshops where they made shoes or cloth.

A waiter was serving tall glasses of beer and had just offered her one when she sensed the sting of a steady and insistent gaze on the back of her exposed neck. Taking the icy glass, she turned around and felt someone's hot breath on her left ear. It belonged to a man who was suddenly very close, scrutinizing her décolletage. The slight tilt of her body allowed him to see the conspicuous outline of her nipples as they pressed through the silken fabric covering her enormous brown breasts. Uncorseted, they trembled with every movement.

"I want to touch you all over," the man said by way of introduction and she could see wide, well-formed teeth looking out from beneath his mustache in a genial, complicitous smile. "Not bad for a white boy," she thought as the music began and he encircled her waist. There was no way to resist. Behind her, the crowd blocked any retreat, and on either side, the towering stranger's arms surrounded her like a prison. A crooner with a high-pitched voice imitated Gardel singing *El día que me quieras*. As the bandoneons gained momentum, she felt the man's body press against her own, which was nearly folded in half over his arm.

And so they danced without stopping. During the most moving tangos a kind of intimacy bound them together irrevocably. Perspiration trickled down her thighs and every time he pulled her close, a mysterious hardness besieged her navel. It seemed as though her breasts were flowing toward her waist, melting into a syrup as orange as the glowing lights of the fringed chandeliers; and despite Nazira's old dress, she felt completely naked, overcome by the hermetic pirouettes of the dance.

"I'm Eugenio Moreira," he finally said as he walked her home. "I'd like to see you again, with all due respect, if you'll pardon the expression. That is, if it's all right with you and your employer." They settled on Thursdays and Sundays: Thursdays would be spent at her mistress's house, and on Sundays he would show her Montevideo because she had barely gone out in all the months since her arrival. It was four in the morning when they reached the dark, deserted vestibule and before letting Angela enter the house, Eugenio Moreira slowly slid his hand into the silk bodice clinging to her damp breasts. It continued downward, the palm stopping on a large, hard nipple. She leaned back against the tile wall and waited as he fell into a kind of trance. Then she brusquely pulled away and went inside, shutting the door behind her.

The following Thursday evening at nine, their long doorway romance began. Eugenio Moreira always arrived with a bottle of anisette for Angela's mistress. They chatted a while in the kitchen, since the family usually sat in the parlor, and then retired to the vestibule on the pretext of saying good-bye. In the five months preceding Nazira's death, Eugenio Moreira never disappointed Angela's expectations nor did she ever stop domesticating his advances through measured doses that reined in the man's desperate passion while keeping him fascinated and docile. By the age of twenty, Angela had discovered the secret source of power: premeditated seduction, permanently controlled through prohibition.

In time, news of Eugenio Moreira's devouring passion reached Angela's ears. Unable to consummate his desire for her, he brought vile white prostitutes to his rented room, but they left him even more unsatisfied. Thus, she redoubled her efforts to secure absolute power over him. One day the high collar of her apron managed to come undone, revealing two egg-shaped black breasts. She allowed him to lean down and with lips stimulated by tobacco and old scars, suck a nipple the size of a tropical fruit. Waiting for him to straighten up, she contemplated a pearly drop of bitter milk that quivered on his mustache. Then she swung around and went into the house, slamming the door behind her. "This little white boy is going to find out what it means to be a black girl's slave," she said to herself as she withdrew to the bathroom.

Her grandfather used to tell her how he had escaped from the chain gang of a thieving frontiersman, down where the devil lost his poncho in Rio Grande do Sul. Parched and starving, his wrists still bloody from the shackles, the soles of his feet torn to shreds, Cristiano Tejera, for so he was baptized by a blind Jesuit, appeared one dawn in July of 1918, looking terrified and shouting insanely: "There is no justice for blacks." Seamstresses hurrying to their shops at sunrise ran away as though they'd seen a ghost. Two sisters of charity, their faces hidden beneath starched linen, knelt before him, reeling off paternosters and begging forgiveness for all the sins of humanity.

That night Cristiano Tejera slept in a cell in the foul-smelling basement of Montevideo's police headquarters. Years later, a guard recounted how he had uttered prophetic philosophical discourses on man's ingratitude, hypocrisy, egotism, and mean-spiritedness—all in his sleep. Once awake, he carried on unintelligible conversations with the rats.

After leaving prison, he became a preacher. At night, a phosphorescent halo sparkled in his fanned out hair.

A kind of latter-day Abraham, he leaned on a crooked staff, like the ones used by shepherds in ancient times, and wandered through the streets of downtown, stopping at corners so pedestrians could toss coins into a bronze washbasin retrieved from a garbage dump. A self-styled pilgrim of life and seer of destinies, he was beyond intentions—both good and bad—going wherever the maritime city's winds might carry him. "From mere washerwomen, prophets are born," he used to say to anyone who questioned his curious occupation.

❊ twelve ❊

THE FOLLOWING DAYS held unprecedented excitement for Jeremías Berro. Though there was no further word from the rebels, his zeal was sustained by a hope that envisioned a new world somewhere beyond his own person, his family, and even his business: by the very capacity to imagine and imagine oneself transforming something more than aromatic substances.

His early morning departures took on an enigmatic air, with no sign of the usual summer high jinx. He spoke very little, bought the newspaper every day, brought it to the café, and, sitting next to a window, read with knitted brows, as though searching for eternal revelation between the lines. He learned that summer was worse than expected in the countryside: the land surrounding the ponds was cracked and splitting. Overworked and exhausted, old livestock was being left to die.

A whispered summons traveled by word of mouth, rallying support for "*the battle to restore the liberties violated and the institutions overturned in the events of March 31, 1933.*" But huge headlines in the February 2 *Morning News* proclaimed: *Subversive Movement Liquidated.* They were accompanied by an "official" account of the most recent action: in the area called Morlán, the first skirmish with insurrectionist forces led by "*possibilist strongman Ovidio Alonso and his contingent of eighty men*" had resulted in total victory for government forces. The rebels—having abandoned their leader, who was shot several times and gravely wounded in the hip—were now holed up in the hills.

So they weren't content to characterize them as merely disloyal. "Cowards" were even more despicable.

Jeremías Berro rubbed his hand across his face. His head was suddenly heavy with exhaustion. He had no desire to lose his new-found reason to exist, the drive to make something of his life. Images of Turkish military impressments flashed through his mind. At night the soldiers forced their way into the clustered homes of the poor: they were looking for Jewish boys of ten or twelve, youths old enough to serve as canon fodder for the troops of Sultan Hamid. The Syrian secret police, the Mukhabarat, would ask: "*kim-bu Yemil?*" His cousin, hidden in a well. His cousin's brother, suffocating in a warm oven. "Let's run away to Kurdistan," they said to one another in the middle of the night. "No, America is better."

No one ever came back from the Turkish army. They were found dead, tied to trees by the officers on duty, frozen solid and emaciated after going without food for months on end. Fourteen years old. "There's a boat carrying vegetables and dried fruit in the harbor. It leaves for Dakar tomorrow."

Four in the morning. Jeremías Berro kisses his mother, his sisters. He carries a small blue knapsack—someone gave him shoes with the soles still in once piece. His grandmother blesses him and his mother gives him a charm that will protect him for the rest of his life. He crosses the square, taking cover behind benches, blending in with the shadowy cedars. His face feels the wind's cold invitation. Please don't let the sun come up yet. There, lowering its ramp, is Nissim Kaleb's skiff, loaded with bags of pistachios, dried figs, sour apricots. The eleven-year-old boy clutches two gold medallions in his fist: one was to be his sister's dowry and the other had been a gift from his grandmother to his mother. Jeremías Berro comes face to face with the old man and opens his palm. The medallions shine beneath a calm, impassive moon. Nissim greedily accepts them and they disappear inside his rags. "Climb aboard," he says, "Get under the pistachios. Hurry." The launch rocks like a cradle on the black Mediterranean and moves toward a cargo ship. Jeremías Berro remembers the pressure of ten kilos of nuts upon his back and the strong, lugubrious smell of the sea.

On Sunday morning Jeremías Berro encounters still more headlines: "Rebel Attempt Languishes in the Face of Public Indifference." Further down he finds some new adjectives: they refer to "a movement without a banner," "a disaster," "a makeshift plot." There are some casualties and more than one hundred rebels have been detained. The core members have been imprisoned on Isla de Flores. Among those arrested, a certain Keleman, and another, Fisman Polak, appear to be gringos like himself. Does anyone know them?

Berro continues reading: "In the meantime the government has complete and open public support." What does that mean? Telegrams from the Association of Patriots, the Radical Colorado Party, and the

National Party come next. Political assembly without the express authorization of the Executive Power has been banned.

"Come now, my friend. What's this worried look all about?" There stands Isaac, nicknamed "el loco," looking down at him from atop his uncommonly tall frame. "May I join you?"

Jeremías Berro does not want company. He needs to spend his time thinking about what he should do in light of recent events.

"Have you been ill?" Isaac asks and then orders a seltzer mixed with claret.

"No," answers Jeremías in a foul mood. "You never know how things are going to turn out. What can I say?"

"Hmmmm," the other one thinks to himself. "What things?"

"How should I know? Whatever will be, will be. This is a strange country. Something that seems unstoppable, unleashed by a legitimate need for justice, comes to a complete standstill because the majority of people are profoundly indifferent. What do you say to that? And then there's something else I don't understand: an anachronistic drive to save face, to pull back when the other team starts to play. 'Every man for himself.' It's all very civilized, but supremely conservative."

"I don't know what you're talking about, Berro. Football or politics? And since we're champions on both fronts, I'd rather you wouldn't bother to explain. Get a load of those two at the other end of the room. There's something about the way they look that says it all. How's the Mrs.?"

❊ *thirteen* ❊

FROM THE DAY NAZIRA first rented that run-down old house on Ituzaingó Street, they referred to Peralta as the man who lived in the cellar. Their landlord, a fat, talkative Neapolitan, made it very clear that the house came with a tenant. What is more, he was entitled to use the family bathroom, which was the only one in the whole place anyway. Realizing this unusual arrangement could bring the price down and eager to exchange life in a tenement house for something that was "just for the family," Nazira accepted the deal.

They brought in their furniture, some kitchen equipment, and several bundles of clothing tied up in old bedspreads, but only a profound silence—one that became more and more difficult to explain as time went on—issued from the basement where Peralta supposedly lived. Throughout that whole first month no one was seen either en route to the bathroom or emerging from the basement stairwell, and Nazira began to wonder if the Italian had been pulling her leg. Jasibe didn't think the tenant existed (or ever had). Lidia, the one who came home the latest every night, assured them the phantom boarder never surfaced from his abode while they were all asleep. There hadn't been any signs of him in the bathroom. But unless his bodily functions were somehow altered to allow for an eternal continence, it was impossible for him not to go there, and in order to do so, cross the patio, walk by the kitchen, and wait his turn in front of the tall narrow door to the "private sanctuary," as Jasibe liked to call it.

Camila had the privilege of being the first to set eyes on him. She was certainly the one who spent the most time at home. Her sisters gave her the simplest household tasks, since she was born slightly retarded—at least according to the midwife in Aleppo. Her diagnosis was later confirmed by a folk healer, someone Nazira consulted when the girl had a high fever that couldn't be cured with the juice of stewed marshmallow plants, taken on an empty stomach. Whenever she went out, she would forget how to come back home.

Peralta popped up suddenly, like a hallucination. Camila was making a mantilla, mechanically linking semi-circles of yarn with a thick crochet hook, when she felt the pressure of someone's gaze against her long hair. She looked up and saw what appeared to be a beggar—a figure deformed by layer upon layer of colorless, oversized clothing that dissolved his body into a shadowy smudge. Two sunken eyes were all she could see of his face. A tangle of gray hair covered everything else from forehead to chin.

Camila screamed. And screamed again when the vision disappeared. "It's the tenant, the tenant," she repeated. Nazira rushed down from the attic, but despite her haste only caught a glimpse of one stooped shoulder slipping into the bathroom as the door closed behind it.

Somehow relieved, Nazira and her daughter waited for the man to come out so they could introduce themselves and maybe even offer him some Turkish coffee. They sat in fellowship for what would turn out to be a very long time. They were still out on the patio when night began to fall and Jasibe came home from the leather goods shop. And when Lidia arrived after dark, her feet swollen from a day's worth of standing, she found the women sitting at the same posts they had assumed earlier in the day. After six hours everyone agreed it was time to open the bathroom door. Perhaps having fainted the man was unable to call for help. Perhaps he was ill and lying on the cold crumbling tiles. The opening of the door had suddenly become a question of the most basic humanity.

They never told the story to anyone, not even to Esterina, who worked nights and came to visit during the day. It was like a secret pact. They had cautiously opened the bathroom door, turned on the little light, and found the bathroom to be utterly, disturbingly empty. No one said a word. The house remained silent, everything in its place, as they gathered around the table in quiet meditation. The subject of the tenant didn't come up again until the following week, when at the start of one otherwise unexceptional morning, he emerged from the cellar as though it were the most natural thing in the world for him to do. He had come to introduce himself and meet the family.

His name was Peralta. A zoologist who specialized in the study of ophidians, he didn't seem to have any family and his marital status was indeterminate. Standing there in his plain, baggy, peculiarly meticulous clothes, he appeared to be quite slender. Nazira offered to do his laundry. And if he ever needed anything to eat, she would make it for him. Yes, he admitted, sometimes a bit of domestic assistance was in order. Lately his studies were taking up all of his time and he had neglected his personal hygiene and nutrition. The girls scrutinized every detail of his appearance. "He's a crazy old man," said Jasibe. "Poor and filthy," decreed Lidia. "I've seen him before," said Esterina, but she couldn't remember when. The only one who remained silent was Camila.

They agreed on a bathroom schedule for Peralta: five in the morning, before the family awoke and eleven at night, after they had retired. In the meantime, he was to leave his dirty clothes in a basket in the kitchen and Nazira would wash and iron everything and leave it all on the basement landing. He could then just pick it up every morning on his way to the bathroom. So things worked out quite nicely. The family could count on comfort and privacy when using the facilities. And the same held true for Peralta, who spent the whole day studying anyway.

No one dared inquire where his support came from, but that detail was the landlord's concern, not theirs, since they were only renters themselves. The vague mention of an inheritance from his late uncle in Tacuarembó adequately explained the situation to women who couldn't support themselves without working. The man, for his part, didn't bother a soul. His cellar was a place none of them needed to enter.

❊ fourteen ❊

THE STORY BEHIND Jasibe's obesity remained a mystery until the house had been vacant for years. Though Jeremías Berro neglected the wife God gave him, sticking her in a corner like a piece of old furniture, she refused to be destroyed by conjugal tragedy. Instead of pining away, she chose to explore exotic flavors. Everything from an elixir of roses—soak the petals in purified water until they are well macerated, then submerge them in alcohol, letting the mixture rest in a tightly sealed container so the vapors can permeate the crimson pulp—to one made of violets, dozens of bouquets bought at the market and transfigured in the kitchen.

Once crushed, the flowers released their tiny souls. Jasibe watched them rise up over the pots—diminutive spirits floating on a trail of steam—before saying farewell. If it was indeed true that sooner or later they all came back, reincarnated in new bodies, then her labors hastened the process a bit.

Narcissus could become a cake stuffed with fragrant pale yellow meringue, vast, soft, and fluffy. But the anemone—ah, the anemone, with its solitary eye gazing at some tired illusion—*that* was the best. The petals of violet and blue, the curved, sinewy stem, the poignancy of an organism born for seduction, languishing with the passage of time, reminded her of the stories of women who were aging the way she was—advancing slowly, calmly toward death.

While engrossed in cooking, Jasibe heard music and chanting from ancient times, sensuous melodies that hummed in her ears. As the exquisite taste of flowers touched her palate, the songs recounted tales of enchantment, adventures in spun-sugar palaces, where syrup dripped from enormous apricots and flowed in sweet, slow-moving streams.

Suddenly a prince of Smyrna would arrive on his Arabian stallion to kidnap her from the kitchen, beckoning with sweetmeats and dates dried beneath oriental suns. Or Sultans with golden eyes and luxuriant beards would invite her to go flying on vermilion carpets that could soar high above the minarets stained dark by an evening sky.

Jasibe ate slowly, as though fulfilling an ancient obligation, and felt each mouthful descend through her body and produce the pleasure of all pleasures, that singular moment of satiety, born of the urgencies described in Eden. She ate like someone who slowly devours the experience of the world and transforms it into her very being.

Therefore, it was hardly just a coincidence that the moment a black market profiteer showed up at her door—a small crippled gringo selling almonds, hazelnuts, and dried fruit from house to house—Jasibe discovered passion. Every Thursday, around eleven, she waited for him to arrive and, hardly bothering to exchange a word, invited him into the darkened parlor. There he would open his cardboard valise and offer up the forbidden fruits. She chewed with ritual care, all the while looking gratefully into his eyes. Afterwards, they would lock themselves in the bedroom Jeremías Berro avoided ever more frequently. And there they would remain until the chirping of caged canaries brought on the dawn.

Years after the members of the family went their separate ways, they discovered that the *contrabandista* had taught her to savor the taste of figs and raisins by placing them all over his body. Jasibe would then lick his grotesque form—anointed with unctuous honeys—from head to toe. It was as though she intended to devour him, introduce his entire being into her own, now grown huge in pursuit of absolute felicity. Very few people would ever know such celestial flavors existed on earth. Rather than accept the lot of a scorned woman, Jasibe drank from chalices containing the elixir of life.

❊ *fifteen* ❊

AROUND THREE OR FOUR in the afternoon, with Camila safely installed in the dining room—brightened up by Nazira, who in an effort to ornament her surroundings, always covered the dark secondhand furniture with tablecloths and runners made by her daughters—

Angela Tejera, dressed to the nines, her hair carefully pulled back beneath a bright red hat, left the house without saying a word to anyone about where she was going or with whom.

As for Nazira, she was off on one of her liturgical visits to the cemetery. Though her parents were not buried in that hallowed ground, she liked to imagine they had been laid to rest there and awaited her presence in order to reconstruct the events of an abrupt separation. For the past thirty years no one had been able to determine what became of them after fanatical Shiites attacked Aleppo's Jewish quarter. Her mother and father had literally vanished from the face of the earth—or they were among the unidentified bodies found shortly after the fire in the Synagogue of Light. Even their deaths were denied a place among the ashes, denied the most minute compensation for lives of endemic misfortune.

Being so very empty, the house whispered its own secrets, some of which Camila understood but could not express. And there were others she preferred not to even hear because of an inexplicable secret dread. Though fifty-four years old, she still looked like a child, unscathed by life. Her feeble-minded expression and limited vocabulary served as protective armor against calamity. That is why she wasn't alarmed by Peralta's sudden reappearance. His clothes were still baggy, but thanks to Nazira, at least they were clean. He was still terribly scrawny, and that face, with its tragic gray eyes peering through cascades of silvery hair, remained as inscrutable as ever, making it impossible to determine his age.

"You, you," he insisted in an anxious voice. "Come downstairs with me; I want to show you something." Camila looked up from her work—a four-needle stocking she had already knit and unknit three times—and stared blankly at him. "Come on," he said in a raspy voice, "this is a part of the world that's just for you."

Something in Camila's mute expression urged him to approach

the armchair, help her rise, and slowly guide her toward the patio. Her pace was measured, like that of a little girl taking her first steps. She leaned on his arm, which was just a bit below her own since he was quite short, and they descended the small wooden stairway to the basement. He courteously went ahead to open the heavy metal door. "Be careful," he warned, "the threshold isn't very high." She bent down and entered the cavern's damp shadows.

Though its ceiling was low, the chamber was wide, and misty prisms of light, all warped and faded around the edges, came in through a ventilator that opened onto the calm summer air of the street. The place was empty except for a conglomeration of cubicles, placed side by side, right next to one another. Some were large cases of colorless glass, their lids made of the same material and perforated by small round air vents. Others were big greenish flasks with pieces of leather covering their small orifices and held in place by knotted cords. Inside, an odd assortment of ophidians rested in curious still-ness. The exhibit offered up a confused spectacle, half laboratory, half circus. At times it seemed to be no more than the den of a care-less collector of exotic specimens.

"Try to comprehend what I'm saying," Peralta said to Camila as she stood bewitched in front of each container. "They're fascinating animals," he repeated, emphasizing every word. "I don't know if you can understand me. Their quietude is deceiving. It's as though they were waiting. And at any moment, at the least sign of carelessness, now follow me, they could strike with deadly pleasure." He contin-ued in a deliberate tone: "They rise from death with a powerful en-ergy and their bite can drag you down into the nightmarish provinces from whence they came."

Camila was watching a one-and-a-half-meter ivory and brown *yarará* slowly glide over its own coils to reveal a pale green ventral surface that stretched interminably toward a dark head with a cross on it. "This is the most beautiful of all the poisonous snakes," enthused Peralta, "a genuine cross viper, *Lachesis Alternatus* of the family *crotalidae*." Camila turned to look at him. The explanation brought a fleeting adolescent warmth to his customarily impassive and ageless face. Even Camila, despite her muteness, managed to express a touch of emotion.

They moved from vessel to vessel with Peralta describing the attributes of each specimen.

The coral snakes were the smallest, marked with every possible combination of alternating red and black rings. The rattlesnakes were covered with brown diamonds, their bodies as thick as human arms and twined around blackish tails that split into overlapping arcs. But the most dazzling, according to Peralta, were the *Mussuranas*. They wore olive green scales on their backs and yellow ones on their bellies. Their most outstanding feature was the tendency to eat other ophidians, even those of a superior size.

As Angela Tejera would learn much later, that visit to Peralta's cellar initiated critical changes in Camila's life. True, she remained almost completely mute, but her eyes glowed as though she had perceived strange new dimensions and incorporated them into an invisible archive. Peralta's love of ophidians unleashed a kind of passion she herself never could have imagined. And when the rest of the family was out, she visited the basement with ever greater frequency.

❊ *sixteen* ❊

THERE IS NO TRACE of the slightly stale smell that always lingers in those warm, consoling witches' dens known as kitchens. Angela Tejera leaves it all behind her as she enters the cool night air and hurries toward Sarandí Street to see the last Carnival procession of the year. It thrills her to imagine being caught up in all the excitement, to be packed in with anonymous crowds of children perched on their fathers' shoulders and held back by rows of box seats, to watch black musicians (and white ones in black face) march by carrying banners that long ago honored the betrayed spirits of the jungle.

Her pace quickens. Dressed in a flowing skirt and Roman sandals, she looks like a goddess emerging from some impenetrable, lacustrine wilderness. People are already squeezed together on the sidewalks; and down past the pushcarts filled with sweets and streamers, the deafening heartbeat of drums rises up from tenement house patios.

The parade begins with haughty pasty-faced señoras, all very white, in tulle headpieces and matching dresses embroidered with sequins, spangles, and beads, perched on top of chauffeur-driven, open convertibles that move slowly and silently, as though suspended in mid air. Wearing condescending smiles, the passengers toss confetti and perfumed streamers to one side and then the other. Allegorical floats are next, bearing huge figures whose limbs swing back and forth, high above the applauding multitude.

And finally, with the vibrating rhythm of tabors comes something Angela Tejera has waited all of her life to see: the black dancing troupes. Sweepers, as tall and thin as men made of wire. Bearded folk healers clad in black tailcoats, spinning their satchels in wide arcs. And old women, all dressed up to perform the *candombe*. Forgetting their ancestral roles as wet nurses to the white babies of pale, dry mothers, they dance with French parasols beneath the sunless evening sky.

As though in a dream, Angela Tejera suddenly sees an image of sloping paths in a Bambara village in the Sudan. Tall women balancing oval pitchers on their heads descend toward her in single file. They wear tight orange dresses that expose one dark, shapely shoulder. Next little girls come with pots of grain and, forming a circle, dance and sing in a chorus.

Centuries later they will be black laundresses, rising at dawn to walk barefoot on frozen pavement while carrying enormous bundles of starched linens on their heads—like pagan queens overthrown by a foreign god. Their clan's totemic kinship with panthers and gigantic lizards will be forgotten, the souls of their ancestors extinguished in the misguided excesses of the world. Angela watches the women scrub and scour the clothing to make it whiter.

Seated on the cracked, dry sand of an empty watering hole, a large Yoruban woman in a blood red turban tells her a tale of Africa. Once there was a beautiful princess, descended from the royal clan of Dahomey, who had all-seeing eyes and hair so long it brushed her feet. She married a sleek golden leopard, and their union was represented by five claws tattooed on the royal family's crest and into the living flesh of its offspring. One night, white hunters chased the leopard into a trap and killed him. Ever since then, on evenings when the moon is full, the phantom princess, transparent and dragging a long, wild mane of hair, roams the jungles searching for her leopard's spirit. An entourage of twelve-legged spiders as big as toads accompanies her and predicts the future of any adventurers who cross in her path.

Angela Tejera hears voices. Fearing arachnids, she touches her arms to search for bites and sees women giving birth to intelligent animals with crystalline eyes—lions, baboons, crocodiles. She hears the roar of a waterfall, nearby cataracts breaking against the rocks. The din grows louder as the sinuous procession winds and unwinds like a snake. Overcome, the dancers invoke their lost *orixás*, attempting to reincarnate them, bring them back to life. Angela looks at her arms, her ankles, and sees the scarring of chains on her wrists and neck. She sees her grandfather, the preacher, engulfed by the threshold of a house, in a maritime city, on the shores of a strange land. It is cold.

❖ *seventeen* ❖

THE MINUTE HER DAUGHTER Alcira turned thirty, Lidia set out to acquire a son-in-law. Alcira looked exactly like her cousins and, generally speaking, like all the women in that interminable family: creamy white, satiny skin, wavy black hair, a sharp nose, and dark, close-set almond eyes surrounded by mauve circles. But she wasn't as lucky as the rest. Her father died when she was only eighteen and from then on she worked as her mother's assistant pastry chef at the parties they catered for wealthy families.

The process of locating a husband for Alcira consumed Lidia's energies for years. The tradition of marrying her off to a brother's son was frustrated by an America that disdained such rituals. And besides, Nazira never gave birth to any male offspring. The women who hired Lidia to run their kitchens at holiday time all had solid, good-looking, olive-skinned sons, but these young men scoffed at their parents' ways. They no longer spoke Arabic, and the only Hebrew they knew was a phrase or two memorized in childhood. None of them would stake his future on a penniless spinster, especially one who evoked a dismal world they all—with good reason—wanted to forget.

And yet, the new generation put plenty on the line at Montevideo's public dances. In this arena they gambled with more than just the destinies of young men practicing at masculinity. There were also the compromises involved in being the first to live a life without any past: to be just one more face in the crowd, a promising civil servant or zealous business man who conducted himself with casual deference and no trace of an accent. Distanced from their parents' fear of exile, strangers to the terrors of hunger and poverty, the cocky "Hebe" upstarts donned the latest style—a gray hat carefully adjusted over the brow—and went out on the town. Young men with Moorish faces frequented the gambling dens of the moment and played cards with hypnotic concentration. Their tough look came from a startling blend of audacity mixed with a dash of arrogance. Women found the combination irresistible.

Nevertheless, Lidia was insistent and, thanks to the occasional matchmaker who complained that her services were unappreciated in America, finally managed to locate a fiancé for Alcira. Though he was almost prepubescent—a mere boy, trained to be a presser in a tailor's shop—his smooth dark face, with its narrow eyes and protruding nose, inspired confidence. His family (who had settled in Paysandú) agreed to the union as long as the meager dowry was turned over immediately; and to close the deal they brought the lucky bridegroom to Nazira's house so his future in-laws could supply him with a job and a place to live. No matter how beautiful and indifferent she might be, a fiancée of a certain age had no right to pretensions.

For seven years Alcira had secretly awaited another man—who seemed not to exist—carefully and patiently inventing him as she scrubbed the floors of her uncle's shop and hurled soapy white streams of water onto the pavement every morning. As the years passed, Alcira honed and refined the physical details of his identity. Ageless, he had transparent pupils and an unmediated gaze that could comprehend her state of mind without a single syllable being spoken. A man of few words, because he came from a place where everything had already been said. At night, just before she drifted off to sleep, he would flow through her mind like warm oil, penetrating her most intimate thoughts, using them to initiate strange conversations about the world, about a simple, nearly forgotten happiness that he and Alcira would reinvent. They spoke without moving their lips, as though praying.

Throughout the years their nights were filled with exotic journeys. They plunged into waist-high warm, salty waters, explored undiscovered cities, and roamed the planets spinning around hidden galaxies, returning each morning, exhausted, to say good-bye just before dawn would break, and with it that thing called day, reality, deception, conspiracy. Adventurers of the soul. Pilgrims of the body. Traveling through one another, they fabricated dreams. But now, with the time of heartless betrothals upon her, Alcira realized she must bid farewell to this imaginary man just as she would to her own lost youth.

One usually killed oneself piece by piece, decisively laying aside the dismembered parts. The day arrived for a surgical amputation, chosen almost without complaint: vulnerability, that suppuration. Alcira felt the restless organs within her womb. She heard them grumble—assailing and coercing her with insolent voices. Something wanted to be born and could not wait. No scruples. The time had come. It was human destiny to give in, to copulate, propagate, swell up, and envelope something that must wait for the right moment to occur.

And even though a bride-to-be was of a certain age and fresh out of dreams, she nonetheless deserved a proper wedding. The sweet table would welcome even those who had pitied and rejected her. Party preparations reestablished a litany of common sense in Alcira's mind: recipes for walnut rolls and date jellies. This marriage would make it possible for the itinerant lives of aunts and uncles, grandparents, and great-great-grandparents to settle down at last in a permanent dwelling place. From beneath the nuptial canopy festooned with orange blossoms, certain character traits—"that boy was always just like his uncle"—would regenerate sagas of happiness and bring back the sheltering world. Like all married women, Alcira recreated the sensation of belonging to a separate dimension, whole again, bound to the past and to the future by ties so firm, absence could never weaken them.

❊ *eighteen* ❊

JEREMÍAS BERRO'S MIDDAY MEAL required the deployment of every utensil in the kitchen. He expected service at his table. And fresh flowers. Burnished leaves artfully arranged to cover the empty stretches of tablecloth between the plates. Enormous white pyramids of rice and basil accompanied the first course; and chickpea stew, sprinkled with a mixture of ground radishes, garlic, and walnuts, waited its turn as the second round. The scent of anise and ginger wafted from sky blue bottles waiting on a sideboard, their fragrant presence reserved for long post-prandial conversations around the table.

Seating was always the same and Camila was always the last to arrive—or be brought in by Lidia's agile hand. Jeremías Berro approached his lunch with an air of concentration, like someone performing the ancient ceremonies of a forgotten ritual. Soaking a piece of bread in oil, he thanked the Lord for his benevolence in permitting the daily pleasure of the meal that was about to take place. Angela Tejera would diligently serve the food and then watch Berro eat with his mother-in-law, wife, and sisters-in-law: one man surrounded by a fake harem of hard-working women. She noted every imperious gesture.

He had refined manners—who knew how such politesse had been acquired in Aleppo?—always pausing to savor his food. And so conversations moved along at a leisurely pace, subject to his expressions of approval or disapproval. The ladies were expected to stay silent while he had the floor, waiting until his observations were complete before timidly responding with a word or two of their own.

Their eyes looked on with a mixture of prudence and dark rebellion as Jeremías Berro ate. He moved automatically, accountable to no one for his actions. Cowed, the women watched for a sign of approval, some tribute to the flavor. Finally, as though in absolution, Jeremías Berro would condescend to offer a bit of praise—always sparing and directed at his wife's massive bulk—for one dish in particular. And though Jasibe nodded and humbly lowered her eyes, she knew, and her mother and sisters knew, that the compliment applied to all of them, all those who shared the inviolate world of the kitchen, undisturbed by men.

Even back in those days, Angela Tejera had no idea how many relatives actually lived in the house. She tried to keep track of their comings and goings, their routines; but it was difficult. She knew that Nazira was incredibly old and did nothing but assign household chores to everyone else. To Esterina, the one who worked nights and slept during the day, she entrusted the job of keeping the tile, pewter, and pots and pans all gleaming. Lidia, who worked from noon until dusk, took care of the plants and the patios, fed the canaries, and kept the bathroom spotless. Jasibe and Angela were responsible for midday meals as well as the preparation of sweets, marmalades, and preserves. Knitting, mending, and ironing were Camila's since her persistent mental deficiencies kept her housebound.

But there were other relatives, and children of relatives, who came and went without Angela recognizing any of them. Afternoons of *narguile* and anisette could include more than twenty guests: some were old—very, very old—and mumbled unintelligible benedictions; others were nursing babies hanging from their mothers' corpulent necks; and still others were prepubescent brothers and cousins who never stayed put in one place.

They all talked at the same time, in deep voices that seemed to rise up from their stomachs. Those aspirated H's were formed way inside the gut, and no one, not even Angela herself, could imitate them.

"What language are those ladies speaking?" she asked.

But nobody ever answered. Instead they invited her to "have some anisette" or "come learn to dance." The next thing she knew, Jasibe would be pulling her out of the kitchen, insisting that she remove the apron and take down her hair. Then, placing Angela squarely in front of her, face to face with that hulking body, she would demonstrate the proper movements, swinging her hips, slowly, rhythmically, from side to side. The cousins (seated on huge pillows they themselves had embroidered) provided a noisy, uneven chorus to accompany these afternoon pleasures.

By then, Jeremías Berro had already been at the store for two hours. The women, old men, and children were free to enjoy themselves, at least until nightfall, which arrived very late during those hot sticky summers. Angela never really figured out why Nazira's family would suddenly explode with raucous merriment for no apparent reason. All they needed was the clapping of hands, arms raised on high, swaying to the beat; and in an instant everyone would be dancing, leaving their cigarettes to slowly burn down on the rim of an ashtray.

Life might have gone on this way—outside of the house, work's daily grind, fear and insecurity, the physical exhaustion tied to a worthless world's alienating tasks, and inside, that voluptuous feast of joy and good food, a sumptuous gluttony meant to warm the passing years and cushion life's sorrows—if Camila had not started acting so strangely. One evening, around midnight, Angela was awakened by a noise coming from the other side of the wall, a soft scratching sound. Her tiny room opened onto a dark corridor that led to the bedroom shared by Lidia, her daughter Alcira, and Camila. The noise would stop for a few moments and then start up again, almost in sequence.

Since Angela slept in Nazira's room (and kept the door locked to protect herself from the abuses of don Jeremías), she decided not to disturb the old woman's rest for such an insignificant nocturnal disturbance. But the following week, and on the very same night of the same day of the week—Sunday—she again heard what seemed to be a rodent sharpening its little claws. This time she got up, tip-toed over to the door, and drawing back the bolt, opened it just a crack to study the dim passageway. There was nothing there but petrified old furniture. Lidia's snores rumbled behind their half-closed door, but Camila was not in the room. Through the darkness, Angela Tejera thought she saw snakes with human faces slithering across the empty bed. Shadows suggesting strange and unusual forms.

At seven the next morning a surprised Angela found Camila already awake and seated in her usual chair. An embroidery hoop was on her lap, but the hands holding it were very still, and she was staring off into space. Angela brought in her usual breakfast—hot celery tea and a dry cracker with fig jam—but Camila remained immobile. She spoke to her, saying: "Is something happening, doña Camila?" Silence. She repeated the question. The woman's lips made an effort to respond. They twisted and trembled, but no sounds escaped. "What is happening to you?" insisted Angela, touching her head. She was feverish, bathed in fresh perspiration. "The ch-ch-ch-hild," Camila mumbled. "The child," she repeated. Angela helped her drink the tea and placed small pieces of cracker in her mouth.

Though not quite sure why, she avoided mentioning this incident to the family. Something told her that Camila needed special protection. There were more Sundays when the noise came just as expected at midnight and the dark hallway looked empty. With time, Camila fell into a puzzling state of muteness. Of course, she had never been capable of delivering well-modulated sentences, but now even the most elementary phrases seemed to tax her limited powers of speech. Angela became more and more solicitous of the pale, mute fifty-year-old, accompanying her silences, her capricious wanderings, her desolation.

Around the third month Camila's stomach began to look distended, as though she was suffering from indigestion. But Angela suspected something else. She figured that with loose dresses and shawls they could conceal the pregnancy until at least the seventh month. Camila was so slender and her body so stunted, no one would notice anything peculiar until the last minute. And since she spent hour after hour at work in the rocking chair, her own knitting and embroidery would help hide the unseemly protuberance that kept her from speaking.

❈ *nineteen* ❈

FOR YEARS, perfumes had functioned as adequate stimuli, motivating Jeremías Berro to study and appreciate an aspect of life that was forbidden to others. But this same apprenticeship predisposed him to the finely calibrated pleasures of inventing special new formulas—fragrances designed to resonate through a woman's olfaction and spark dramatic changes in conduct. It was madness. He discovered that a certain aroma could produce chaos in human relations: a gradual slackening of decorum, of stiff manners, and an immediate secret connection to the earth's hidden undercurrent. Much of his time was spent observing perfume's disruptive quality. That plunge into the rarely glimpsed brothel of nature itself: an acknowledgment of animality, essential to survival.

Above all, a good extract required sorcery. And time. At least five or six months of repose to allow the subtle *bouquet* to develop fully, because the first inhalation of a well-made product must never be dominated by the smell of alcohol. It was also necessary to avoid filtering the blend of ingredients until at least eight to ten days after first combining them. During this time impurities would form a sediment that settled to the bottom, leaving a clarified potion. Once decanted, tinctured, and aged, the aromas would recapture the essences as nature had created them and they would cling to parched skin like fragrant aureoles.

His Peruvian Amber was made from roses, jonquils, absolute essence of jasmine, yellow amber, musk, and vanilla. Jeremías Berro would let the ingredients rest for more than ten weeks, during which time he spoke to them as though they were living beings. Every morning there were conversations about the flight of pleasure in human lives, with the expectation that at least a few words would permeate the aromas meditating inside the sealed flasks. He was convinced that, in the end, those words would breed surprising transformations and generate perfumes capable of adapting themselves to the cares and desires of anyone who used them.

Essence of Cyclamen, on the other hand, required lilies of the valley, amyl salicylate, liquid essence of violet, balsam of tolu, and dissertations of an energetic, almost violent nature—like cyclamen itself, which could rapidly convert moments of indecision into dramatic declarations of love.

Patchouli was a beguiling scent, pulsatingly sweet and hot on the skin, a balm that restored charred souls and whisked them away to the Orient. Lost in its fragrant spell, one saw white walled palaces with arching doorways. And inside, the soft bluish light of an amphibian world where silent, silk-clad women, bewitched by the glow, floated across endless carpets of swirling arabesques.

And so the perfumery's back room became a site of permanent effervescence. Its elixirs wafted through the tenuous lives of sweethearts, mothers-in-law, female companions, and hopeless spinsters who listened faithfully to radio soap operas. They enveloped secretive men who undressed in the privacy of their own bathrooms and spruced themselves up for other men. And they accompanied solitary transients as they walked to work, dreaming of a dip in the fountain of youth.

But now, thanks to his unforeseen contact with the young rebels, a far wider expectation had attached itself to Berro's energy (though daily headlines kept his enthusiasm from going overboard). The Tartaglia boys had said someone would be contacting him about a special mission requiring his unique skills.

From that moment on, he did nothing but wait and hope to hear from them. Even his erotic reveries about Angela Tejera, if not completely abandoned, gave way to another recurring dream. It always started with him slashing his way through a riot, wielding a huge cutlass in defense of the Uruguayan patriots of the Río Negro who had already defeated several official regiments and were now fighting to liberate Montevideo. The balconies looking out onto Avenue Dieciocho de Julio were filled with people waving the banners of past freedom fighters like Lavalleja and Artigas, applauding the victorious revolutionaries as they marched through the streets. And Jeremías was right there with them, saber in hand, on the back of a wild stallion.

Nevertheless, by Thursday morning the headlines looked grim. The *Morning News* announced, *"Revolution Ends as Last Cell of Dissidents is Dispersed."* And the *Daily* said, *"Complete destruction of the group commanded by Basilio Muñoz is now confirmed. The wounded leader has escaped."* It grieved him to see all the telegrams supporting the government, to read about the large bands of citizens who had volunteered to help the militias.

Jeremías Berro's brief utopia would have ended right there if two weeks after the catastrophic newspaper reports a dark, raw-boned stranger had not shown up at *Perfumes of Carthage*. He was poorly dressed, his face partially covered by a woolen scarf, and said his name was Isabelino Giménez. The Tartaglia brothers had sent him to ask Jeremías for a very special favor.

"Don't believe what they say around here, my friend," the man implored in a slow, grave voice. "Propaganda can't wipe out a movement like ours. I'm telling you, don't believe a single word. The game is just beginning. It's the truth, but I don't know if you're getting my drift."

He continued in a whisper: "Listen, my friend, how about making some explosives? We want to blow up certain key locations in the capital. Do you understand? Something impressive, a major assault. A bomb that can be thrown if possible, and really powerful, my friend. Death to anyone who sides with that fucking dictator. That's what the patriots want from you. And as soon as possible, because the movement from Brazil is losing momentum. Montevideo must not be left on the sidelines. You understand that you have to do your part. It's time to send a clear signal to our *compadres* in the capital. Those starched-collar types who are all talk and no action. You get me? Guys who don't have the balls to take this fight out into the streets, where the only thing that really counts is courage."

The speed with which the man appeared, explained the request, and then disappeared (right after agreeing that he would contact him within a few days) left Jeremías Berro feeling simultaneously excited and overwhelmed. But his enthusiasm soon turned to confusion. Was he really in any position to manufacture an explosive device? In a fragrance laboratory? How was he supposed to know about the workings of something like that? And who was expected to plant all those explosives in strategic pro-government locations? He could see that a number of points required clarification, and yet, it still seemed worth a try. At the very least, he would convince the patriots that he was on their side. And perhaps, later, after the movement had triumphed, they would assign him a more dignified job. He could supervise a huge industrial enterprise dedicated to the production of oriental perfumes. Turn them out on a grand scale for the people of the interior. Wouldn't gauchos want to smell fresh after a hard day's work in the fields? Wouldn't revolutionaries be the first to realize that true change in vernacular society required an alteration of aromas? How could any kind transformation take place without the lingering cadences of purple carnation mixed with essence of geranium? He would create the scent of a new world. It's very breath.

The bomb had to be produced as soon as possible. "Death to those who side with the dictator," he remembered Isabelino Giménez saying. Then the goal was to build something that would do more than just explode. It had to be lethal. He felt a slight shudder in the pit of his stomach, beneath the convex belly jutting out over his belt and past his suspenders. It had never been his ambition to belong to an army that expected its members to be "capable of killing." If anything, he had gone to the opposite extreme, seeking out life in all its sensuality. Despite the imperfection of the world's crafting, its insufficiency, he had known the aroma of happiness. And that was no small matter.

Nevertheless, he worked for three days and nights, absorbed in the alchemy that would produce the desired results. All for nothing. It seemed that neither coumarin, nor vanilla, nor the essence of orange blossom would ever generate a substance flammable enough to explode upon impact. Besides, Angela Tejera's breasts still beckoned him. Life was so full and its pleasures had taught him so much. How could he ever stop filtering and simmering aromatic essences? It was as though in some strange way they exuded a certain harmony. He found no satisfaction in the image of an anonymous, random, public demise. It made him think of medieval engravings of demiurges, with Death's skeletal form reconnoitering the crossroads, lying in wait for unsuspecting pilgrims—poor nobodies felled by chance. If he could choose his moment, he would want a personal, intimate death. And he wished the same for others. "The end should be as light and translucent as an aroma. Impalpable."

❈ twenty ❈

THERE WAS NO BETTER TIME than when figs and dates chewed indifferently between swallows of syrupy café Moka filled the mouth with emphatic sweetness. Afterwards, scattered sediment in the bottom of the bowl would disclose our uncertain human fate.

Mornings had a kind of suddenness because the midday meal required sleight of hand as well as industry. There was something miraculous in the way dusty, telluric elements, extracted from the bowels of the earth or from the insides of greenish, uterine fruits— seeds on the verge of bursting their skins, buds sprouting with tiny leaflets—could, after undergoing the occult processes of the kitchen, become enormous platters of hot rice enhanced with red pepper furbelows. Steaming wonders surrounded by the golden halos of heavy aromatic sauces. Miraculous that such a feast could come from hands reddened by icy water, the fingertips ugly, swollen, and cracked: little gnomes, slicing, squeezing, grating, coming and going of their own accord, detached from arms, autonomous.

Shrine-like fires licked but did not burn them. Hot oils coated but did not penetrate them. Fruits touched but did not stain them. Their rich colors—those beets, those radishes—merely left behind a faint, almost imperceptible, violet glow.

Mornings led to lunch as though to a secret garden, an Eden that needed to be rescued little by little with the gathering of roots, bulbs, and stems, one by one—enjoining the grocer not to give us scraps exorcised from a heap of putrefying rejects—in order to reconstruct paradise, always pristine and perfect before the advent of human beings. It was hands, and feet shod in wool knitted on four needles by hands, and more hands. It was full skirts and pin-tucked aprons tied around prolific bellies that gave birth to extraordinary meals, day in and day out.

Then came the afternoons. A different rhythm. Afternoons took their time, clinging to the remains of lunch. There was no desire to press on toward evening. Instead, they seemed to stretch themselves backwards, trying not to occur, reluctant to notice the events of the day. Knitting, radio soap operas, cards. Tea with orange peel sipped between shared confidences and recipes. But now the kitchen was a salon of advanced aesthetics. Only the finest liqueurs, only walnuts dusted with powered sugar, only almond roulades soaked in anisette. Now hands could pause to enjoy the pleasures of delicate patterns, sumptuous embroidered filigrees, turbulent flowers and fruits, and last but not least, the consecration of colors—mauve, so deep, dramatic. . . .

Women. Full lips, large breasts, hair tinted and precariously coiled into place with tortoise shell combs and gold-plated barrettes. And lace blouses embroidered in adolescence beneath the watchful eyes of mothers and grandmothers. Women whose bright smiles revealed broad, sturdy, slightly yellowed teeth. They discussed their neighbors, their neighbors' daughters, their nieces, their nieces' daughters, their nieces' daughters' neighbors, their nieces' daughters' husbands. Talking and sewing, talking and knitting, talking and chopping, because something was always on the verge of happening: a meal, a marriage, a birth, an anniversary.

Everything but a divorce. Since time immemorial, no one in the family had ever been divorced. Yes, there were some widows, but they all found second husbands. And nobody got divorced. Some had even tolerated being locked up for days, arbitrarily starved and punished by arrogant, villainous spouses. Still, marriage remained an impregnable institution, a fortress where living together and children justified almost everything that went on inside its walls. Compatibility was not required. Men and women were brought together on the advice of a matchmaker, and a rabbi's benediction transformed them into beings capable of those fifty or sixty years of strange fidelity.

Flavor was another matter entirely. A paste of ground sesame seeds and sugar had to be dry enough not to feel oily or crunchy in the mouth. When stuck to the teeth and palate, its taste and texture were sheer bliss. The same high standards applied to walnut bonbons, glistening like tiny opaque prisms bathed in translucent honey. Such gustatory gems were to be savored slowly. The time for flavors was absolute, blameless. Those diminutive liqueur-soaked pieces made their way right to the very center of a person's most intimate sanctum: the stomach. Gut deep, it was another heart, emitting emotions by means of gases, fermentation, and satiety. Their convergence produced something akin to happiness.

Dried figs and golden dates also had to be included. Stuffed with almonds and dipped in syrup, they looked like small bits of glazed ceramic, almost woven. Resistant to the bite, they produced a kind of modesty. Rough and sweet, tart and pure—their effect remained long after jaws and daily domestic strife had ground them to a pulp.

And the liqueurs. Served to aid digestion after the large midday meal. Or at six in the afternoon when the languid summer sun set in wise resignation and clandestine joy, knowing that tomorrow there would be another day, one more. Crystal clear anisette, clouded by the pale breath of opaline goblets. Rose-petal liqueur, aged in wide bottles—remoras spilling perfumed blood. A sudden fire burned the throat and children would ask what was happening. A huge flame, sharp as a dagger, traveled down, down, finally plunging into the pit of the stomach where it released a bucolic warmth. And then one would have reached that distant horizon, the vast space of limitless joy.

❋ twenty-one ❋

ALCIRA STARED AT HERSELF in the oval mirror above the dark second-hand bureau. It was her wedding day, and the red bridal gown ignited a silhouette which the glass split into three imperfectly superimposed figures, blurring the image slightly and making it glow.

Three entwined amulets hung at her neck: a lidless eye of blue crystal that sparkled whenever she moved her head, a silver filigree hand to ward off the destruction of the world, and, hidden in a red silk pouch, a small clove of garlic to guide the newlyweds along a safe path.

And yet, the bride was not afraid. "That's just the way things are," she told herself. "I have to get married." She examined her eyes, searching for a hint of rebellion, a touch of defiance. But no. The groom didn't really matter for the most part. She would still set the table every noon and make supper every night. And listen to his stories (it made no difference whether they were boring or exciting). She would be that place called home, the place to which one could always return from one's wanderings. Nothing less. And ultimately, a hub, cranking out baby after baby, each one pushed into the future by dreadful mysterious forces.

Nevertheless, the mirror hesitated to sharpen the image of Alcira in her wedding dress. Better that way. She dreamed she was as light as a bird, supported by frothy clouds. With no possibility of falling. The vermilion veil cascaded down from the top of her head like a crystalline curtain, and there were flowers embroidered by her Aunt Camila on the gown's demure bodice. Perhaps even her face had been transfigured while she waited to be summoned downstairs for the ceremony.

Below, conversations and congratulations blended in with the sounds of hurried footsteps, chairs scraping along the floors, clinking china. It most certainly was her wedding day. Alcira looked at herself again. The heavy black hair pulled back beneath the veil created a dramatic frame for pale skin and high cheekbones. Her family's deep mauve circles made the face recognizable once again. Glancing down she discovered a greenish flask on top of the bureau: "Dreams of Aleppo." Uncle Jeremías had prepared it especially for this occasion. She struggled a bit with the wide cork stopper, and after finally releasing it, raised the bottle to her nostrils.

A dizzying burst of almond and sandalwood flooded her brain. It was like a mind-altering surge of electricity. She closed her eyes for a moment and saw the silhouettes of women—Arabs and Turks— enveloped in black silk *charchafs*. They walked with measured steps beneath the leafy almond trees of a tranquil, exquisite park. Opening her eyes, Alcira glimpsed a strange image in the mirror: it was her own body swathed in a black silk *charchaf*. And above the veil, her own eyes, larger and darker than before. She quickly closed them and found herself on the back of a creamy white camel, its hooves tinged a pale yellow, just one of many in a long caravan headed for Persia. Passing through the oasis of Haman, they found a garden overflowing with grape vines and fig trees, and a superabundance of pomegranates in full bloom.

As the line of camels moved on, commanded by a slender bearded Arab with long gray hair tucked under a red fez, Alcira inhaled the potent fragrance of tangerine and orange trees. Prodigious globes swung back and forth on the tips of their bountiful branches while women shrouded from head to toe approached the caravan and offered up bright golden fruit, saturated with honey.

They are on the outskirts of Aleppo. There is no doubt about it. And her great-grandfather is the one organizing a rest period for the men and their charges. She follows along, invisible, translucent, back in the seventeenth century, untouched by distance and the death of missing relatives. It is May. The farmers of Hamah have begun to harvest the cotton. Uncontaminated by evil, a cold, white torrent spills from the oasis.

She opens her eyes but the perfume's aroma remains undiminished. She sees another silhouette in the mirror: a smiling old woman with the gums of a toothless child. It is her great-great-grandmother, Sultana Gaón, the one who raised thirteen daughters and wet-nursed countless abandoned babies. She is sending her best wishes in an ancient French spiced with Hebraisms: "Mazal, mazal. Heureuse mariage." Her eyes sparkle. (Alcira is surprised to discover a minute tear trembling in the corner of one.) Behind her great-great-grandmother a poor neighborhood slumbers. Small, squat houses, surrounded by high stone walls. It is Aleppo's Jewish Quarter. An intense aroma floats up from the jasmines entwined on its rooftops like perfumed tapestries.

Her toothless great-great-grandmother recites a story:

"Long, long ago, when warriors laid waste to the mountains and none of us had yet been born and none of us had yet passed away and none of us had wept, the Governor of Aleppo tried to transform one of our holy temples into a place where animals and profane gods would be worshipped. But when he raised his hand to give the order to his henchmen, a serpent sprang out of the earth and wound itself around his arm. The ruler understood and rescinded his command. The serpent unwound itself, went back into the earth, and took refuge in the cave of Elijah, there in the very place where he lived and where he became invisible to his followers. Elijah stayed with the serpent for the rest of his days. Ever since then, it has been necessary for all those who seek wisdom and tranquillity—which are not the same as happiness—to descend into Elijah's grotto.

Though Alcira listened attentively, the mirror grew silent and her great-great-grandmother began to disappear. First her hands, then her trunk, then her tightly braided gray hair. Next her cracked lips and small liquid eyes. Sighing heavily, Alcira lifted her gaze. She wanted to expel the perfume and fill her lungs with air. But instead she saw a narrow paved street that rose up and up, curving northward. It was lined with homes whose candle-lit windows revealed tables set for the Passover Seder. White linens, a sudden blaze of sweet red wine, bitter herbs. Seated around the tables, small children with their hair in ringlets watched wide-eyed as grave-looking adults read aloud. Sometimes the little ones giggled furtively, or touched feet under the table. Something had happened thousands of years earlier: the freeing of slaves. A miraculous escape across a stretch of land exposed by the parting of the waves. Wanderings through a desert of sky and stone.

A God spoke to them from on high and said he was One and unchanging. He tried to instruct the liberated slaves, but it was not easy. They had idols, conjurers, false prophets. The God spoke in the midst of an empty desert to people who were searching for a land they had never seen. Shepherds who wanted a deity of flesh and blood, one they could touch. But the God was invisible. He spoke and asked the people to listen, to heed His word.

Gathered around the flickering candles, the children asked the question of all questions. In old Aleppo, where caravans transported pepper and myrtle, children asked about the meaning of slavery, who God was, and why He could only be known through His word. It was Passover of 1724, the same year a handful of Canary Islanders crossed another sea to found Montevideo.

"A God of words," thought Alcira as she ascended the slope toward the market square. The sun had already set behind the mountains of Lebanon and the darkened cedars looked like sacred columns. A Mediterranean breeze was blowing, as it always did after nightfall. Alcira shivered in her diaphanous golden tunic. "That same word produces the blessed and the terrible. How is it possible?" she asked herself. The shadows of ancient stone columns stretched themselves out over Aleppo's marketplace. Alcira was now climbing a flight of stairs leading from the Street of Splendor to her great-grandmother Sofía's house. Gusts from the north tilted the flame-filled lanterns along her path. As she walked through the large semi-circular entryway, an enclosed patio, lush with wine dark roses, miraculously appeared. There, in the threshold of wood and bronze, her three-hundred-year-old great-grandmother stood waiting, hands smeared with honey cake batter, skirts fluttering in the wind. The scent of sweet, sweet early figs wafted from an invisible kitchen.

"Come," she said in a youthful, welcoming voice. "I have some things to show you."

❄ twenty-two ❄

"DON ALEGRE, w-w-we're in real trouble when crim-m-minals like th-th-em c-c-can parade around just as they please on Avenue 18 de Julio, with uniforms and Nazi b-b-bbanners and all the rest, w-w-without anyone trying to arr-rr-rrest them," whispered Beto as he turned off the radio. Autumn had already claimed the morning hours. A weakened sun was shining on bolts of woolen cloth scattered across the tables.

Don Alegre grunted quietly and looked up from his prayer book. Beto's aunt had warned him. Her nephew was talkative and liked to share his dreamy-eyed meditations on current events.

But Carmona hadn't paid much attention to the old lady's words. That poor misshapen young man carried enough bad fortune on his back. There was no point in quibbling over details.

"The Almighty never lets evil disappear completely, Beto. If he did, then what would become of us?" said Carmona, returning to Job.

"Wh-wh-what would become of u-u-us?" repeated Beto, imitating the old man's intonation. "I'm s-s-saying, why should anyone make the effort to be a good person if shit's just going to k-k-keep falling on us from heaven? That's what I'd like to know."

"Enough, Beto," rasped an irritated Carmona. "Don't talk that way about the Almighty. We can only change," he explained, "when confronted by evil in others, and in ourselves." And he flipped through the pages of his book, an 1878 edition published in Smyrna.

"The Almighty, the almighty," mimicked Beto in a whisper, hoping that Carmona would hear it nonetheless. "No one kn-kn-knows him but you. You're the only one who t-t-talks with him. Let's be honest. He f-f-forgets everyb-b-body else. That's the way the world is. So much praying. Wh-wh-what's the use?"

"I've explained this to you several times before," said Carmona, but Beto was already looking out through the shop window again. "His voice tears us away from a certain type of life, let's called it mundane, a kind of animality. Do you understand? Listen to it, and you'll develop a conscience."

"Don't m-m-make me laugh, don Alegre," exclaimed Beto as he went to sit down in the entryway. "The only thing I've ever d-d-developed is this thing on my back," he said pointing to his hump. "S-s-something that doesn't have the slightest connection to God. My c-c-conscience never had a chance. God listens only to you, don Alegre. There are thousands who have never even seen his shadow. Do you understand?"

At that moment, Jeremías Berro's sister-in-law Camila entered the shop. She was wrapped in faintly colored shawls. No one had expected to see her there, silently looking over her shoulder with those eyes encircled in violet. Don Alegre jumped from his chair, because for the past fifteen years, memories of Nazira's quiet daughter Camila—now a faded fifty-year-old woman—had occupied a very special place in his heart. Even though he was already an old man, with an old man's severe disposition, he was nonetheless capable of appreciating her bucolic innocence. Her modest silence. Her reserve toward an indifferent world she never would have chosen willingly.

It was Jeremías Berro, that insidious, sinful creation of the Almighty, who had decided that Camila, though an aging spinster, should not marry a widower twenty years her senior. There were no explanations other than Berro's despotic arrogance when he passed in front of don Alegre's establishment, always turning his face away in an obvious display of sarcasm.

It didn't matter to Jeremías Berro that Camila would waste away in peaceful imbecility for more than a decade of winters filled with homely knitting projects, nor that she would slowly succumb to a kind of progressive muteness.

Alegre Carmona never saw her again. Until now. And suddenly, there she was, standing before him, enveloped in shawls despite autumn's fickle nature, and trying to say something she could not express.

Camila pointed to her stomach, looking alternately at don Alegre and then Beto, as though waiting for their approval. Beto, for his part, looked at don Alegre and then back at Camila. And don Alegre did the same. But neither one of the men could understand her gestures. Finally, Beto leaned forward a bit—his hump looked even more pronounced in this position—and with an air of alarm, slowly approached Camila's mid section. When he was about half a meter away, he extended one timid arm and moved his hand toward her. First he felt the knots of Camila's macramé shawls, then, beneath them, the coolness of a cotton house dress resting on a stomach so hard and convex, it could have been holding a gestating egg. "Ah," said Beto and a bit shocked by what Camila had revealed, turned to look at his employer. Don Alegre could not believe what Beto's eyes seemed to be saying and shook his head in denial. Nevertheless, he made Camila sit down and once again questioned her as to what she wanted from him. Camila sighed, lowered her eyelids a bit, and folded her arms parallel to one another, as though forming a cradle. Then, she moved them slowly from right to left, over and over again, until don Alegre shouted "No!" and growling unspeakable curses, put his head in his hands. "Who did this to you?" he repeated over and over again without really asking, since he knew Camila could not possibly understand the question. "Who got you this way?" he moaned as though someone had driven a frozen stiletto into his very soul.

By way of an answer, Camila lowered her head and placed her pale hands over the womb that stuck out like another stomach when she sat down. Unblushing. Then she raised her eyes to don Alegre again, as though making some kind of plea. "Cloth?" he asked with unaccustomed gentleness in his voice. "Is that what you need, to make new dresses?" he confirmed without looking at her. "And something for the child? Certainly, of course," conceded don Alegre, still in hushed tones. His face twisted in anguish, Carmona instructed Beto to look for what she wanted and to give her as much as she would accept.

An expressionless Camila leaned against the counter and waited for Beto to bring the cloth. Timidly, almost with a sense of embarrassment, she stopped after choosing two or three grayish flannels for herself and a white batiste for the new baby. Beto carefully cut and folded the lengths of fabric, wrapped them in heavy brown paper and handed them to her. Don Alegre was still holding his head in his hands when Camila, in a mute gesture of humility, bowed hers and unsteadily departed, disappearing with slow, small steps into the bustling street.

"W-w-wait. I'll g-g-go with you," Beto shouted as he followed her outside. "You mustn't get lost in the crowd."

❊ twenty-three ❊

"I'VE BEEN DREAMING the same dream for a year," says Angela Tejera as she peels potatoes for lunch.

"Well, of course, young lady," Jasibe responds, "that's what happens when you live in a dream." She is sitting on the patio in a big wicker settee, waving a carved wooden fan at rivulets of perspiration. Her enormous white body (wrapped in a dressing gown that has seen better days) fills the entire seat meant for two. "Have you checked to see if my mother needs anything?"

"I already took care of it. Señora Nazira is actually sitting up and knitting in bed," replies Angela, concealing her annoyance. The curly peels accumulate untidily on a wooden work table in the wide, doorless kitchen.

"But what about her drops?" asks Jasibe, sighing as though she doesn't expect an answer.

"I gave them to her a while ago, when it was time," says Angela in a monotone and then (rather hopelessly), "Can I tell you my dream now?"

"Of course you can." Jasibe slows down the rhythm of her fan and stares off into the shadowy corridor where a bit of light from the street can be seen.

"OK, it's about an airplane. Of course I've never seen one; but in my dream I know it's the kind with three silver gray motors; and the number F31 is painted on the grooved metal body. A genuine airplane, with two rows of seats and around twenty passengers. I see two men operating gauges and meters in front of a dashboard full of switches. I don't know how to explain it, but I see the whole interior of the plane without being inside of it. Kind of like a ghost, watching what's going to happen without being noticed."

Angela stops. The knife blade has slipped and cut the tip of her thumb. A small drop of blood appears. "Damn it," she whispers and holds her finger for a moment.

"Continue," Jasibe says softly, her eyes half closed. "And what *is* going to happen? Those men are the pilot and copilot. Where are they off to? Your dream is putting me to sleep."

"I don't know for sure. The plane is always in the airport, about to take off. Through the little windows you can see other planes taking off and landing. Lots of movement. The dream begins when they start the engine. There are problems. The motors make a terrible sound. It's all happening in another country."

"And where is this country?" Jasibe asks as though in a dream. The fan's hot breeze lifts her curls for moment.

"I don't even know its name. It's not too far away. A big country with huge mountain ranges. And hot volcanoes. And jungles. The airplane has flown over a crowded city and just touched down. But in the dream, it's getting ready to take off again. Just before it leaves the ground, I wake up feeling nauseated, with my stomach all tied up in knots."

Angela puts the potatoes into a white enamel pot and sets them on the wood-burning stove to boil. She then takes a basket full of broad beans, sits down on a wooden stool next to the work table, and begins to separate them one by one, extracting the seeds and skillfully tossing them into a container of water.

"Well, if the nausea is due to something other than pregnancy, it's a lovely dream. Look here—all that flying must be marvelous," says Jasibe, crossing one gigantic thigh over the over. The fan's rhythm has visibly slowed down.

"No pregnancy, God help me. But this dream isn't a happy one," thinks Angela, now engrossed in the pile of beans on her lap. "On the contrary, ma'am. I tell you some day this dream is going to end badly. That is, if I go on dreaming it."

"So what are you thinking of doing?" asks a drowsy Jasibe as though the conversation is just a way to make the morning move along.

"What else can I do but dream? And thank goodness I can. My friend Demetria, that black girl, says that people who don't dream lose half their lives. Because dreaming helps us live as fully as possible. Do you know what I mean? When will *I* ever get to travel on an airplane? When will *I* ever fly through the clouds to another country? So I'm going to dream as much as I can. And Señora Nazira has admitted more or less the same thing to me: she stretches out her years by dreaming. Don't let her know I told you her secret."

Jasibe looked at Angela Tejera for the first time. She stared at her dark form, hunched over a lapful of beans. She was splitting the pods and removing their contents, her face hidden by a mop of hair so curly it looked like it had been touched by electricity. She started to think about herself and her marriage to Jeremías Berro. Nothing seemed more alien than the ability to dream. When had life become so routine, so full of the same motions, the same looks? And when— without her even realizing it—had he started inventing his own dreams (rapturous ones, she suspected), dreams that excluded her? She felt slightly discredited by Angela's musings.

"We can't all . . . ," she said in a raspy voice, resignedly dropping the fan on her prodigious thighs. "We don't all want to prolong life under any circumstances whatsoever. . . ." She let the last sentence die out and leaned her head back against the settee. Her own mop of barely graying hair was still just as she had arranged it early that morning: one braid piled high and held in place by a huge tortoise-shell comb. Like a gypsy queen. The lunchtime smell of reheated stew floated over the roof of the terrace and in through the open sky-light.

Angela Tejera didn't look up. The potatoes simmered gently, exhaling spirals of steam.

✿ *twenty-four* ✿

RABBI NISSIM ALFIEH was an obese man with rosy cheeks and sad eyes, a combination that produced ambiguous feelings in the visitors who came to him with their troubles. Equally jarring was the contrast between his smooth shiny bald head and curly gray beard. An elliptical pink pate hardly accorded with the prolific arborescence shading his chest. That morning, his wife—a tiny, nearly invisible woman—peeked through his usually closed office door and told him the shopkeeper Alegre Carmona was waiting for an appointment.

Outside in the sparsely furnished vestibule with its two straight-backed chairs and old mirrored coatrack, Carmona heard the woman's whispers punctuated by the rabbi's deep, serious voice: "Serve him some anisette while he waits and bring me my silk robe." Looking out from the third-story casement, Carmona could see an aging gray air shaft lined with the impenetrable windows of the building's other tenants.

Minutes felt like hours. The faded mirror reflected his image: stubborn, lost in thought. It was painful to behold. He hadn't been himself lately. As the years passed by, he thought despair might give way to some other creed, but it was hopeless. His conversations with the Almighty had produced little understanding. What was this painful story that never ended? And who was this God who was unable to relieve him of the world's afflictions? And what was this evil, this injustice that contaminated everything? And this stillborn promise of a better future?

"Let him in," he finally heard the rabbi tell his wife. She returned with a pale face and narrow smile. Carmona padded behind her (afraid he might make too much noise on the wooden floor) and entered the shadowy room. A silhouette blocked the white light of a small window which was flanked on either side by towering bookshelves that seemed to grow from floor to ceiling, branching out as though they were alive. The rabbi coughed from the depths of his belly and invited him to sit down.

There was a strange silence. Carmona didn't know where to begin, and everything he could say seemed too elementary. Finally, with great difficulty he managed to ask: "Rabbi, how do you explain cruelty? I mean those evil people who walk the earth without being punished, without the fear of God, without a bit of remorse?" He instantly regretted having spoken, as though his questions had already been answered a thousand and one times in other places.

The rabbi smiled broadly, revealing a mouth full of surprisingly beautiful teeth. His eyes crinkled up at the corners and began to sparkle.

"Come, come my friend, unburden yourself. There's nothing better than finding the words to name what's ailing us. That is where we find the God who provokes and confuses us, but also makes us grow. Amen. Let's drink to our health," and he poured red wine into two short dark goblets.

"Rabbi Nissim Alfieh," Carmona replied, "thirteen years ago I developed a deep hatred for one of our own. He stripped me of happiness that should have been mine. After I became a widower, I fell in love with his wife's sister. She agreed to be my bride but her brother-in-law, the only man of the house, refused to let us marry. Hoping he would reconsider my proposal, I gave him all my life's savings so he could set up a perfume business and import tinctures and essences. It didn't matter one bit. He never said a word of thanks and never returned so much as a crumb. Every night that womanizer goes to bed with his wife and sleeps like a baby but he has betrayed her in such a way. . . . It makes me sick to say it out loud, even to you. His own relatives have let it slip that he committed a sin with the very sister-in-law I courted so many years ago. Back then she was humble and submissive. They treated her like a servant. And now, he's gotten her pregnant. You should see him parading around all smug and insolent, heaping new sins on top of the old ones, completely indifferent to God."

Carmona rapidly stroked his beard, as though trying to calm himself down. He lifted his glass of wine, whispered "*L' Chaim,*" and drank it all in one gulp, wiping his reddened lips with the back of his hand.

"There's a story I'd like to tell you," said Rabbi Nissim Alfieh, settling down in his chair. "It's a story that happened four centuries ago when we were in Halab. The Talmud speaks of a certain Eliezer, the son of Jonathan. They used to say he'd been to every harlot on earth. Whenever he heard of one, even if she lived in another town, he'd pay her a visit. One fine day, news arrived of a beautiful prostitute who lived in the middle of the desert and collected enormous sums of money for her favors. After gathering together the required amount, Eliezer traveled to the desert to see the woman. When he arrived she made a pronouncement: 'Heaven has condemned you to death.' Eliezer fled from the house and asked the mountains and hills to plead for mercy on his behalf. 'Before we seek mercy for you, we ought to seek it for ourselves,' they told him, 'since it is written: The mountains will move and the hills will tumble.'"

The rabbi leaned forward to serve Carmona more wine. Then he lifted his own glass and with a celebratory gesture took a long, slow drink.

More at ease in his chair, Carmona seized the opportunity to inquire: "Did the mountains and hills speak in those days?"

"Everything spoke and continues to speak to us now," the rabbi responded and then picked up where he left off: "Desperate, Eliezer asked the clouds and the earth to seek mercy for him. 'Before we beg mercy for you, we ought to say a prayer for ourselves,' they replied, 'because it is written that the heavens will grow black with smoke and the earth will fall apart.'"

Carmona listened attentively and rolled the goblet back and forth in his heavy hands.

The rabbi went on, modulating his voice to accord with the circumstances he was describing, "Eliezer went to the sun and the moon and pleaded: 'Pray for me.' The sun and moon replied: 'Before we pray for you, we ought to seek help for ourselves, since it is written: And the moon will be humbled and the sun shamed.' Eliezer realized that no one would intervene on his behalf. 'Everything depends on me,' he cried, and placing his head in his hands, he wept and wept, and the tears relieved his soul."

"Ah," said Carmona in a timid voice. "That passage from the Talmud is just an old story. At the end of his life Eliezer finally repents his iniquities. But the grievance I hold in my heart can't be set aside. Why don't the wicked suffer for their sins? It isn't fair to those of us who are righteous," he said in a lowered voice, a bit shocked by his own words.

"Ask Job," the rabbi responded in a grave tone. "He will tell you."

"Precisely," said Carmona and he recalled the passage in Scripture, "Am I strong enough to wait? What end have I to expect, that my heart should endure. Is my strength the strength of a rock? Is my flesh bronze?"

With a deep sigh Rabbi Nissim Alfieh replied, "It has been said that sin makes wise men human and enables them to guide others. If things weren't so, then no one would be able to tell good from evil, and no one would try to control his own temptations. It may seem obvious to you, but I will say it anyway: there isn't a soul on the face of the earth who has not sinned."

Carmona looked down at his empty goblet and saw the lees of a blood red wine. The subtle aroma of resurrected grape vines drifted upward. Once again he remembered Job: "My complaint is still resentful, and His hand weighs down on me even as I groan." A torrent of water flowed from the land in a place he could not specify: it was the source of the Jordan, rushing down the mountainside. He saw Job chained to the rock, turning to stone. And the sun escaping toward a fugitive destiny. He saw a child, nearly an adolescent, hiding papyrus scrolls written in Assyrian. Then the youth retreated to a valley. "What do you have there? What do you know?" he asked him. And in Hebrew the boy replied from afar: "The life span of the world."

Rabbi Nissim Alfieh adjusted the shabby silk robe over his chest. Against the light of the window, his beard took on a phosphorescent glow. Motionless, he waited for a word from Carmona. But none came.

As though he suddenly heard the unspeakable thoughts plaguing the man before him, the rabbi stood up and said, "Better that the enemy sees my happiness than that I see his misfortune." But Carmona had not said a word. He sat there, silent, head down, staring at the empty glass in his hands.

❊ *twenty-five* ❊

Streetcar number six headed for Rodó Park creaked loudly on the tracks, as though its wheels needed greasing. Every squeal of the breaks sent Angela Tejera hurtling into Eugenio Moreira, who sat at her side, watching pedestrians slide by on the sidewalks. Whenever her body touched his well-built physique, it seemed to send iridescent sparks into the misty May air. Beneath his lowered hat brim, Eugenio Moreira's eyes became narrower and narrower with each little collision.

There were only eight adults on board, along with two children who ran up and down the aisle laughing and shouting. In front, the motorman was engaged in a leisurely conversation with the guard. Angela Tejera nodded off as the car rocked back and forth, her entire body falling into a deep slumber. Their regular Sunday outings followed a ritual that Eugenio Moreira observed with the utmost care: get off in front of the tiled fountain, walk along the pathways lined with elms and eucalyptus trees, follow the shoreline of the lake, and, once in a while, venture out onto the pier. At the appropriate moment, go for a one-hour boat ride. Then peanut brittle or chocolate bars. Afterwards, a fervent declaration of love on the part of Moreira to an indifferent Angela. At nightfall, stop by the tearoom for something to drink or a bite to eat. Next, a slow stroll through the shadows, with fiery caresses on the part of Eugenio Moreira. And finally, the streetcar ride home and farewell until the following Thursday.

At four o'clock on Sunday afternoon, the avenues slowed down a bit and reluctantly allowed a more dilatory pace. The streetcar rolled impertinently through the slums, breaking up soccer games and hopscotch. Near the Central Cemetery's tall gates an other-worldly silence intimidated the passengers. Despite their fleeting pace, they could still make out the dense black groves where spirits of the dead were garrisoned—phantoms from long ago who kept a sharp watch over the living.

Angela Tejera closed her eyes and saw Carlos Gardel seated behind a Colombian pilot named Ernesto Samper Mendoza. They chatted and smiled but she could not hear what they were saying.

Facing away from the pilot, on his right, a young helmeted copilot flipped switches on the control panel. It was an F31 from the Sacol line, ready for takeoff in a country Angela was unable to identify.

They were rounding the last curve in front of the Central Cemetery. Tiny little houses with solitary windows lined each side of the road. Radio music blared through their partially opened shutters. Angela's eyelids felt heavy and began to close involuntarily. The airplane's three engines were warming up. Behind Gardel, who continued to smile as he passed a hand over his brilliantined hair, about twenty people chatted gaily in two rows of seats. The scene was mute except for the movement of their lips. Angela could tell they were discussing various countries: Panama, Cuba, Mexico. It was an artistic tour. They had already been to a few key stops—Puerto Rico, Venezuela—and were on their way to the next city, but she couldn't make out the name.

Angela focused on Gardel again. Now silent, he was absorbed in thought, staring out at the runway. She saw a plane in the distance, tiny because it was so far away. SCADA was painted on its side. The motors were running and the aircraft shook from the vibration. Gardel's face looked solemn, pensive. Angela tried to examine him up close and noticed a shadow fall over his eyes, like a warning. In her dream, she wanted to say, "For the love of God, Carlitos, don't go." But the words wouldn't come. She was mute.

The streetcar was traveling down Gonzalo Ramírez Street, dragging *plátano* leaves along its rails. Kids had tossed nails and coins on the tracks so the passing vehicle would make them smooth and flat. Seated in chairs on the sidewalks, old ladies knitted automatically as mantillas for church materialized in their laps. Angela had again slammed into Eugenio Moreira, who held her with one enormous gentlemanly arm. And again she dreamed of a tri-motor plane warming its engines to take off at three o'clock on a singular afternoon in a strange country.

She read the copilot's lips, "We're taking off." And she saw the airplane go down the runway, gaining speed and ripping through the air like a dagger stabbing into the bosom of the atmosphere. It went up, one meter, two, six and had almost leveled off when a cloud of smoke suddenly rose from the right engine and unfurled in a volcanic explosion over the wing. "Stop," shouted Angela in her dream. "Please, stop," she screamed in desperation, all the while knowing that she hadn't uttered a single sound and that no one was paying attention to her.

"Wake up, *mi negra*," said Eugenio Moreira, shaking Angela Tejera's clinging body. "We're here." He lifted her into the air and set her on her feet. "You've been crying in your sleep," Eugenio murmured in a soft voice. "Who knows what's bothering you. Maybe you're repenting some dark sin—but who can tell," he mused, lowering his head.

❈ twenty-six ❈

THE MISTY MORNING paid homage to winter's remains. From the window of a tavern named The Larks, Jeremías Berro contemplated what looked like the vestiges of a lacustrine city. Trembling water flooded the intersections, its heavy liquid surface barely breaking into ripples.

A steaming cup of ink black coffee sat on the table, and behind the counter shrill tangos blared from a radio. It was 7:30 A.M. and a busboy was scrubbing the checkered floor with a boar-bristle brush.

The Nation's headline struck Jeremías like a thunderbolt: *An Iron Fist From Now On.* Below that, not an objective report, but a diatribe, it's true purpose being to condemn the assault on the President at the Maroñas Racetrack. Fortunately no one was killed. *"With this act of criminal violence, an agent for the opposition has given concrete form to our adversary's state of mind,"* it warned. *"This is no time for le-*

niency. *Yesterday's events must serve as a lesson to the government. The highest circles of power must demonstrate a strong conviction to defend our country from enemies both known and suspected, moving swiftly and decisively against any who would try to take control through violent means, as in the current situation. . . .*"

Jeremías read carefully to see if he could find some mention of a bomb explosion. He searched through the accompanying articles. But no. There was something about a shooting, a bullet that missed its mark. A suspect detained. But the name told him nothing.

Despondent, he folded the paper. It had already been three weeks since Isabelino Giménez had disappeared, carrying with him three explosive devices wrapped in newspaper. After listening attentively to Jeremías Berro's instructions on how to operate them (a whispered exchange in the back room of *Perfumes of Carthage*), he took off for parts unknown. Jeremías's enthusiastic love for the rebels was forced to enter a reluctant phase—with him stepping back as though to view things from a different perspective.

Now, he sat at his window in The Larks and waited for a sign, an omen. Unsure how his contraptions would behave, he had failed to tell Isabelino Giménez the whole truth: when they were thrown, his devices would set off loud explosions—but the blasts would also smell strongly of sandalwood and lavender. He simply couldn't resist adding them to the formula. What is more, he hadn't made a trial run to see how large the explosions would be; thus, when all was said and done, the subject of death remained a question of chance. It was difficult to imagine an impersonal demise—Giménez hadn't told him who the targets would be—which meant several stubborn problems had to be addressed. Under the circumstances, Jeremías Berro felt he could hardly ignore the matter of aesthetics, and so he created a highly combustible mixture that was also profoundly aromatic.

Behind the greasy windowpane, the streets of the Old City, awakened against their will, hid an icy softness. While the busboy continued scrubbing the corners of the baseboards, other customers without shelter came in and sat down at the marble counter. Suddenly, as though responding to an impulse, Jeremías picked up the paper again. He flipped past the larger headlines and lecturing tones without really knowing what he hoped to find. Until his eyes fell on a small box in the middle of the page dedicated to "Police Matters"— just below an ad for cough syrup. "*Strange incident in the Aguada neighborhood,*" he read. "*A man was found dead under mysterious circumstances: killed by a freakish aromatic explosion in a boardinghouse.*"

The victim's neighbors declared they heard a loud blast around three in the morning. They rushed to his room, but found the door locked from inside. Two hours later the police arrived, forced the bolt, and encountered what could only be described as potent fumes of lavender heated by some form of combustion. The explosion had burned the dead man's face and hands. Strangely, no personal effects or clues to the victim's identity could be found among the debris.

Jeremías Berro felt his world collapsing—the world of vindication that had died with Isabelino Giménez. What had become of the Tartaglia brothers? Where were the rebels now? The government was claiming victory because the contingents based in the countryside had failed to show up for a February rendezvous with Muñoz and his men. Many blamed disorganization, the lack of decent couriers. But some matters remained ambiguous, to say the least.

Trembling, Jeremías searched through the flannel jacket that was a bit too small to cover his growing belly and extracted a small newspaper clipping from an inside pocket. Having followed the contours of his body, it was wrinkled, but still readable: "*What happened to the Batllista liberals who supposedly organized the movement? Why didn't they intervene as promised. Where were they at the final moment? Why was General Martínez, who had planned so many things, nowhere to be found? How could the Nationalist Directorate authorize a movement if things weren't ready? What prompted the leaders to leave and get them-*"

selves arrested while driving on the open streets of Montevideo, the very same day as the outbreak?"

Questions kept floating through Jeremías Berro's mind. He closed his eyes in hopes of a revelation and saw a group of three hundred men camped in the shade of a eucalyptus grove. They were bathed in sweat, waiting for the predicted military insurrection. In vain. He saw night fall over the woods, and the horses, freed of their saddles, shaking their tails at a watering hole. And the men, trying not to look at one another. Some, just boys, crying in the darkness.

Suddenly, from out of nowhere the scene of the final evening unfolded before his eyes. The bristling silence as owls hooted ominously around the encampment. The measured breathing of sleeping men. The pensive vigilance of those who abandoned hope as the night wore on and of those who divined evil spirits and treacherous ghosts among the trees. Then, daybreak, renunciation, *nada*.

It had started to rain again in the lacustrine city.

❈ *twenty-seven* ❈

THE TRAGEDY OF DON ZAQUÍM SALAM occurred in May. They found him dead, slumped over his desk with a bullet in his brain, blood staining that marvelous white hair. There was a strange message next to the body: the word *cafishio* written in blood on an old newspaper clipping. *The Daily*'s investigative reporter claimed the clipping was from 1925 and read: "*Nine Polish procurers and thirty-five gringa prostitutes arrive in the port of Montevideo.*" The police declared they were investigating a vast network of prostitution and procurement which had managed to survive even after the houses on Yerbal Street were closed down. The rest was hearsay spoken in whispers, quick sprints through patios, the sudden announcement that doña Regina's pension was closing for an indefinite length of time due to municipal reforms.

Alone in her room, Esterina Mualdeb buried her face in her hands. She felt as though a piece of the world was crumbling away. The sagging bed seemed like a funeral bier. She was never to see it again. That man would have nowhere to turn when he wanted to confide in her and express his deep hatred of the world. He may have called himself an anarchist, but she was one too, without even knowing it. The same weariness bound them together. That, and a curious innocence that came over his face as soon as he fell asleep.

Suddenly doña Regina hobbled into the room with a still-sleeping Lunita in her arms. "Take her," she said between gasps, "I can't do anything for her now." And in a dry, broken voice she began to recount a story of tragic love: "Once upon a time, many years ago, one of those *caftans*, you know what I mean, fell in love with a prostitute. She had picked up an illness from someone who passed through without leaving another mark on her. This *caftan* tried to buy the girl, because her owner, another procurer, had tricked her into leaving a small town in Belorussia to come to America. Out of sheer cussedness—money didn't matter to him—he refused to sell her, shipping her off instead to a bordello out in the country, on the outskirts of a wild town named Viyela, a place that doesn't even exist anymore. 'Heartless cruelty,' as they say around here. The lovesick pimp searched for two years until he finally located her whereabouts. By then, Raquel, may she rest in peace, was already dying from the infection, wasting away on a filthy bed infested with lice. He lifted her up like a rag doll—she weighed only forty kilos—and took her on a two-month voyage back to her native town in Belorussia.

"They arrived just as night was falling—it was winter—and they walked through that miserable sinkhole toward her home; but instead of the farmhouse and cowshed, all they found was a scorched, cracked piece of earth, empty except for some twisted scraps of metal. The Ukrainians had massacred her family. There wasn't a Jew left in the whole village. Seeing this devastation, the girl, only eighteen years old, dropped to the ground and begged the man to kill her. She wanted to be buried on that very spot. Moved to pity, he complied with her request. Then he returned to Montevideo, found her former owner, and stabbed him ten times, one wound for each of the commandments."

Esterina placed her sleeping child on the bed, gazed at her for an instant, and then took down the cardboard suitcase from on top of the wardrobe. If she arrived at Nazira's house at this hour of the morning it would cause talk and awkward questions. But she had nowhere else to go with the little girl.

Her childhood in Aleppo was definitively behind her now: bright summer sails illuminating the evening sky, succulent vegetable soup, hills of browned rice. She had learned to choke back fragility and live in a world made of stone, where faces, old age, and disenchantment counted for nothing. A world indifferent to death and that final slide into the abyss.

They said she should go to Buenos Aires. Hell was substantially larger and more complicated there, where it was still possible to get by unnoticed and engage in personal self-destruction in some gloomy hole on the outskirts of town. The kind of place that attracted toothless old men with callused hands, old coots happily dumbfounded at the sight of a "French girl." Assumed identities made it easier to avoid explanations. In America, biographies were condensed into labels—"the Russian," "*la negra*," "the divorcee"— and worn like borrowed clothing. The women quickly stopped telling their life stories, those small tragedies that all sounded the same, babbled between drinks and bursts of laughter. The repetition of sorrows, heavy bodies, stigma. It had all been summoned up years ago and tucked away outside of time. And space.

For ages now conversations had been restricted to just a few topics: infections and consultations at the Dispensary about personal hygiene and cleanliness. And the weather: an unusually dark, rainy winter. Esterina Mualdeb surveyed the landscape through a small foggy second-story window. Below, the bustling street looked the same as always. Don Zaquím Salam was no longer around, but the morning still vibrated with its usual routine. She thought about his white beard and remembered the smile filled with big yellow teeth—now flashing in eternity.

She was about to take Lunita in her arms when she thought she caught a glimpse of him below. The anarchist. On the sidewalk, facing the door. He was leaning against a banana tree and seemed to be waiting for her. The profile was the same: long mustache reaching down to his collar bone, arms crossed over his chest, betraying a certain impatience. Esterina Mualdeb picked the little girl up with one arm and held her against her shoulder. Then she grabbed her valise and purposely made the loudest racket possible as she descended the stairs—for the very last time.

❊ *twenty-eight* ❊

THE OLD LADY was almost always sleeping—transported to who knows what premature other worlds—but Angela Tejera spoke to her anyway. She couldn't allow things to go on in secret anymore, as though it was all part of some double conspiracy. Just a short time after she discovered and hushed up Camila's strange pregnancy—fifty-four was practically old age when it came to the demands of giving birth—her own blood seemed to disappear, stuck in some capricious corner of her mysterious belly. And the worst part of all was that it too had begun to grow autonomously beneath her apron.

She would tell Nazira what was going on: how everything had happened on the streetcar when she was asleep, leaning against Eugenio Moreira's shoulder, with Carlos Gardel on the verge of taking off from an airport in some strange country. She would tell her the truth: that no one had ever touched her, that she was truly a black virgin; and heaven had sent her a pregnancy to make up for all the afflictions and sufferings of humankind. Obsessed with this higher purpose, Angela Tejera prayed at the secret altars of Demetria's African great-grandmother and begged the Oxum of fresh-water rivers to allow her to beget reverence, and not infamy.

After penance, cleansing, and purification, after fasts and the sacrifice of a fat, noisy old chicken in a heavy, fragrant broth, Oxum responded through the casting of *buzios*: Angela's paths were entwined with those of the loving river spirit who carved her way through the plains that once, long ago, belonged to Yoruban kings. A seductive woman combed her hair in front of an oval looking-glass, her translucent skirts submerged in the quiet waters of a slow-moving iridescent stream. Gentleness of a purely fictitious nature—because an ordinary glance failed to take in the whirlpools on the bottom, the unforeseen pull of malignant currents mixing water and mud into an elastic magma where sticky midstream death awaited the gullible. In the meantime, Oxum combed her hair beneath a lunar mirage and hid her face under cascades of pearls streaming from a silvery crown.

She rose and found Nazira dozing on her white pillows, her unbraided hair spread out like a fan—dry, discolored, but still abundant. Her hands, resting on the sheet's exquisitely embroidered hem, looked like works of art, as though someone had carefully shaped and transformed the shallow depressions of her bones into tiny masterpieces.

Angela would tell her little one (the baby she hatched in her head before the gods placed it in her body) how she had met Nazira: "Why all the tears, my child," asked the slender white woman who smiled with her eyes and walked along the street like a pilgrim, carrying bags of vegetables through the vacant lot where Angela had dropped down to cry over her misfortunes.

"We don't take blacks here." That's what the man said—the butler who worked for the family they sent me to when I left Topacio. Do you know the town? It really doesn't even qualify as one. Well anyway, the idiot never imagined a black girl, the daughter of slaves, would descend on them. You could see the family was rich. A villa on El Prado with three dogs who sniffed at me like I was another animal. No one cared that I have nothing to go back to: "Look across the street, girl." No place to go. They put my aunt away the same day I left town. There's no one left in the houses there. Not even ghosts.

Then Nazira—I didn't know her name at the time—spoke to me in her *gringa* accent. "Come with me, my child. I have some fried rice that will make you lick your fingers." I asked if I could help with her bags; but it was really just to be polite since I was already carrying them as though they were completely weightless and an invisible angel was pointing the way home. That was months ago and now Montevideo is even more brutal than it was when I first arrived.

"Be well, doña Nazira," whispered Angela, not wanting to waken her. "You can see that I'm pregnant, but listen, it's not because I've sinned. Oxum wishes to make amends. Do you follow me? That is, unless the baby's father is. . . . I don't really know how to say it, because you're going to think I'm making it all up, that I'm some kind of screwball with big ideas. . . . If I tell you, if I dare to say it, I know you won't mention it to anyone else. You'll take it with you to the grave. What I mean to say, doña Nazira, is. . . . Remember how an angel put me there on the street right in front of you? Well, another angel brought me to him. But since he's far way and we'll never meet, I found him in my dreams, and it was in my dreams that I became pregnant. Yes. I have to say it. Look, whether you believe me or not, the father is Carlos Gardel."

❊ *twenty-nine* ❊

DON ALEGRE CARMONA opened his eyes at the top of an arid plateau, but God's face was not there. Just His word. The hills rolled downward, tumbling over one another between shallow depressions of red stone: lethargic valleys where icy torrents flowed for millennia, only to be sucked dry by the thirsty heavens. Brownish dust outlining the contours of an infinite, faceless God. Unless the eroding fissures, the intricate trails in the sand, the capricious topography happened to conform to a certain visage, an assemblage of recognizable features, something like an intention—there could be nothing more than the word. "Pay attention," the landscape seemed to say, "Human beings must listen carefully."

But all he could hear was silence. In an effort to decipher it he slowly scrutinized the panorama's wide horizon: to the west, the mountains of Judea, reddened by solar rust; to the east, the overwhelming desert plain with its colorless, undulating sands—after nightfall, a motionless sea, carved in plaster. To the south, the path that encircled the Earth, always returning to its point of departure.

Perhaps it was this hatred for Jeremías Berro, amassed over the years and scrupulously stored in his heart; perhaps it was this contempt, coagulating over time, that kept him from hearing what God said to common ordinary people like himself, like his assistant Beto. A hatred so refined it became the determining factor in a deliberate decision to get things over with once and for all, so he would at last be able to return to God, to hear God's word.

Nailed to his stool, facing the greenish, moisture-stained walls of personal prisons, don Alegre Carmona explored his mute visions with a desperate longing to hear the word. He wanted God to articulate the meaning of the world again. His fundamental purpose. The reasoning behind injustice. Some consolation for all the pettiness and cruelty.

"D-d-don Alegre," droned Beto out in the store, "it's time for your *m-m-maté*, if I'm not m-m-mistaken. Should I m-m-make it?"

Don Alegre heard Beto's voice, but it seemed far away. He blinked. The green stains reappeared on the wall. The desert of colorless sand had vanished.

"Don Aleg-g-gre," Beto called out again. "Do you hear m-m-me. Are y-y-you all right?"

Time was up and God hadn't said a word. Disconsolate, don Alegre Carmona rose from his stool, barely strong enough to stir his body and get it moving again. Beto was standing off in the distance, behind the two glass doors. He didn't look human. A marionette controlled by slender connections to a powerful secret mechanism no one could understand. He felt fragile, forgotten.

"The w-w-water's hot now," said Beto very softly. "Should I p-p-prepare it?"

An ancient scribe once wrote, "The word is very close to you, it is in your mouth and in your heart, that you may live by it." But Alegre Carmona had not been able to find the word. Not even inside of himself. God's mute, he stood there, adrift, watching Beto through the glass doors.

❊ *thirty* ❊

"PLEASE WRITE THE LETTER," begged Angela Tejera in a low voice. She was asking for the third time now, pleading with Jasibe's enormous shape as it paced up and down the hallway. A strong aroma of minced garlic had invaded the corridor where the older woman's ever-expanding figure lumbered along in slow motion, dragging her shadow's vague outline through the semidarkness.

"Why do you want to write to him?" Jasibe asked, now stopping in front of a big pot of azaleas.

"To warn him not to travel, that he mustn't go traveling. I know what I'm talking about," said Angela, her voice breaking slightly.

"Gardel? Carlos Gardel?" she asked incredulously.

"Yes, him, the one and only," replied Angela between sobs. "If you don't help me, he's going to die."

"Well, all right, I'll help you," Jasibe and her shadow finally replied as they used a kitchen fork to aerate the soil in the flower pot. "I may not know how to write, but I have a good memory. You tell me what you want the letter to say and I'll make sure Peralta, down in the basement, writes it for you. We'll mail it to his record company, RCA Victor. They'll deliver it to him."

"Good. Tell him to be careful about traveling on Monday the 24th. Tell him not to get on any airplanes, especially in countries whose names start with C. He should never even visit a city with a name that begins with C. Tell him I dreamed the end of my dream. Around three o'clock on a calm afternoon, a chartered three engine plane takes off from an airport in a strange country, mountainous and wild. Gardel is on board with his whole entourage: three guitarists, an English tutor, and some other people I don't recognize. They're rising in the air, seven or eight meters off the ground, when the plane suddenly twists to the right—something has gone wrong with the brakes or a wing—and it crashes on top of another that is about to take off with twelve people on board, the poor things. Gardel is sitting behind the pilot. One of the motors crushes him and everything bursts into flames. It's an inferno. I can't look. Gardel's body is reduced to ashes. His smile, gone forever. I hear a radio: 'Carlitos has been killed.' I see a huge crowd walking toward the port. A ship, a coffin. Then I wake up, drenched in sweat. I think I'm pregnant."

Jasibe was sitting in the wicker settee, her huge breasts splayed across her belly. She had heard enough to understand.

"Pregnant! Are you sure, young lady? I told you Eugenio Moreira couldn't be trusted, my child. Didn't you see it coming? A gaucho on his way up, defiling an orphan. It's positively shameful what's happening in this country. No one gives a hoot for anyone else. Well, things will be different when I get my hands on him. He'll marry you. That much I guarantee. He's not going to do this to you, or anyone else, ever again," concluded Jasibe in a sententious voice.

"No, no. You're getting it all wrong," Angela quickly said in desperation. "It wasn't him. He's never laid a finger on me. And I've never touched him or anybody else. I swear it. All I wanted to do was make him my slave, grind him under my heel. Doña Nazira will tell you as much herself. A handsome self-promoting white boy like Eugenio. Touch me? The pregnancy came from my dream. The dream I've been telling you about. It's Gardel, his spirit. I swear by the jungles of my great-great-grandparents that spirits exist and have superhuman powers. Didn't the Virgin give birth to Jesus through the spirit. I swear it's the same with me, ma'am. I dreamed the same dream for months because the spirit had his eye on me. And who knows on what unguarded night of grace he chose me. He didn't want to die without having a child. I tell you, he didn't want to pass away like that, pass away without someone to redeem him. I'm absolutely sure. Gardel's the one—the only one it could be."

❊ *thirty-one* ❊

THERE WAS A PLACE in childhood where one was infinitely happy. That is what Cristiano Tejera preached on Montevideo's street corners the day of his two hundred and fourth birthday, just before he died. More than an actual place—said the old people who remembered having heard him—it was a boundless space that increased and grew at will, spilling out over a deathless horizon. Years later, his granddaughter Angela Tejera was scrubbing the curved stairway at the entrance to Nazira's house on Ituzaingó Street. Autumn had already penetrated the morning—albeit obliquely, almost reluctantly. Cristiano Tejera had disappeared without a trace, as though his body weren't composed of matter, and he only existed as a voice thundering inside his granddaughter's brain. She listened without wanting to.

"Babylonian nights," said her grandfather in grave tones. "That is what will come." Then there was a slight pause, during which Angela Tejera tossed her head from side to side as though shaking out the old man's obsessive chant. "Everyone will talk to themselves and no one will listen," he continued. "There will be nothing but a din of empty, automatic words," he proclaimed. Rebellious, Angela willfully scrubbed the vestibule with even greater zeal, an attitude stemming more from irascibility than meticulousness. The ancient voice kept on speaking above the commotion made by Leyland buses and streetcars and the honking of Chevrolet convertibles as they stopped at the corners to drop off dramatic-looking ladies swathed in gray fox. A world beyond prophecy, thought Angela Tejera, a world that would soon become absurd.

Suddenly she saw people running toward Sarandí; a huge crowd was gathering a few blocks up the way. Cars were hemmed in by pedestrians and the horses harnessed to ice wagons had come to a complete standstill. Town criers were silent, but a growing wave of whispers inundated the street. Standing in the doorway, she heard a radio: "Gardel is dead. His plane crashed in Medellín. We are orphans." Throwing the scrub brush on the stairs, Angela Tejera began to run. The sidewalks seemed interminable. Her apron strings fluttering at her sides, she finally reached the insane tumult of people in the plaza and fell down on a strip of faded grass to cry. She saw yellow bursts of flame enveloping the beloved face, pale with surprise and attempting to rise when the massive burning engine fell on top of it. She saw plumes of black smoke twirling upwards like the Devil's greedy breath.

After that, nothing would ever be the same. Her grandfather would never preach in her ears again. The world would slowly unravel, and its tattered shreds, attached to meaningless things, would float about randomly, carried to and fro on the winds of the sea. Were she to say that her grandfather Cristiano Tejera was a preacher and a prophet at the age of two hundred and four, people would look at her with skeptical eyes and laugh condescendingly. Black washerwomen carrying bundles of white linen on their heads would pray for her pregnancy at household altars. She would be a black widow, dislocated in time, and never dance again.

❋ thirty-two ❋

FOUR MEN with impassive faces. One fatter, another taller, but all wearing gray hats banded in black, pulled low over the same motionless features. They appeared in the vestibule on the very day Camila found it impossible to get out of bed. She lay there beneath her yellow blankets, curled up like a pale, phantasmal larva. Much later, Angela would recall how she barely had a chance to open the door before they charged in and pushed her aside, one of them waving a piece of paper so close to her face, she could hardly make out its official-looking seals and flowery signatures. The patio seemed to grow smaller in their presence, and the canaries became frantic, taking off on short flights that sent them smack into the rusty wires of their cages.

"OK, where is he?" inquired the one brandishing the paper. "Where is that clever little creole?"

Jasibe came out of the bathroom in a threadbare robe—her pink carcass still warm and damp, slender wisps of steam spiraling up from her hair—and froze in front of the meager door.

"All right señora, let's see if we can make this any easier," the man continued with a touch of irony in his voice. "Where are you hiding that mafioso?" As he spoke, the others were twisting and turning their heads, perusing the ceilings, the walls, the skylight.

"We're the only ones here," Jasibe managed to say in what she hoped was a polite voice. "My mother, who is asleep upstairs, and my invalid sister. And the maid. You can check for yourselves, if you wish." As she spoke she wondered what had become of Jeremías, who had been gone since seven that morning.

"Don't try to turn the tables on me, señora. You can see we're gentlemen. Now tell us where the hell Peralta is and we'll leave you in peace."

Wringing her hands, Jasibe sighed deeply and, with a look, directed Angela to show them the way. Angela watched the men descend the steep little stairway, gather together at the bottom, and break down the cellar door with a few kicks. A fetid odor came up from below and rose through the patio, now immersed in a violet light that looked like dust floating in the atmosphere.

At first all they heard was a fearful silence, then rebukes. Finally piercing shouts cut through the stinking air like a knife. Footsteps, running, heavy objects being moved around, then dragging noises. Jasibe and Angela were still frozen in front of the bathroom door when the first heads peaked out from the stairway. They were towing two men the women had never seen before, their faces swollen and disfigured (the eyes almost completely shut), arms twisted behind their backs, tattered clothing hanging from their mournful bodies. Held up by the other men, they looked like specters emerging from deep inside the earth to wander through purgatory.

The man who shook the ominous paper spoke without moving his lips: "We haven't found Peralta," he said, "but these two will be enough for now, señora. And don't tell me you didn't know two foreign anarchists were hiding in your house. We may even have to take you in," he snickered while tugging at the end of his thin, well-trimmed mustache. "Unless you call me as soon as Peralta returns. And you'd better not forget," he warned in a harsh voice, "because we remember things like that. Do you understand me?" he added, looking her over from head to toe.

"Yes, of course," Jasibe responded in a soft voice. Her forehead was covered with perspiration and for the first time her body actually seemed small. "Of course we'll let you know," she murmured.

The men departed, leaving a suffocating cloud of coughs, phlegm, and tobacco behind. Just then, Angela heard Camila moaning. Barely able to keep her balance, she hurried up the stairs—sagging from years of unsteady footsteps—and entered the dark nest of a room.

The bed was a confusion of wet rags with Camila's pale form resting on top of them. Her mouth twisted to one side, she moaned rhythmically over what had just happened: a tiny formless bundle lay in the middle of a large puddle that was slowly soaking into the burlap mattress.

The expression on Camila's retarded face signaled a mute tragedy she was incapable of describing. Something had gone terribly wrong. Angela felt the bundle. It was some sort of body, cold and stiff. Despite the darkness, she could tell there was something odd about it. Even in the heaviness of death, a slimy skin covered what would have been a diminutive face with exceedingly narrow slanted eyes. Instead of a nose, there was a protruding muzzle with no lips. It looked like a tiny slumbering saurian.

Days later, when Camila felt better and could sit in her rocking chair, she took part in the small creature's burial beneath the house. Angela waited until Nazira was tangled up in her secret dreams and they could be alone. It was a simple ceremony: a prayer to the *orixás*, an ancient song in Arabic to protect the souls of stillborn babies, and then the soft black earth, moistened by a week of intermittent rain. Afterwards, they lit a sky blue candle in memory of the little soul that, like so many others, had arrived at the wrong time.

CX 32, Radio Aguila was broadcasting the news: Berta Gardés had just arrived at the port of Montevideo and she was mourning the loss of her dear Carlos in front of an emotional crowd. Strains of *The Dying Bird* played in the background.

❊ *thirty-three* ❊

THE PATIO OF NAZIRA'S HOUSE was unsuitable for a wake. There was something about the oblique golden glow that came in through the dim skylight, illuminating the arabesque covered tiles of her uneven floor. Despite a general state of deterioration, the combined effect was festive, perpetually hospitable. Six chairs had been placed around the large, simple coffin made of unfinished pine, and relatives and acquaintances took turns sitting in them so the deceased would have company. In the kitchen and neighboring rooms, old people, wives, and restless children—the latter chasing one another in circles and under the tables—formed groups of four and five. Though silence was the order of the day, one could hear the murmur of an improvised dialect: whispered Spanish sentences spiced with Arabic interjections.

"The dead are still the dead and deserve respect," warned Jasibe, anticipating the questions newly arrived guests wished to ask about the circumstances of Jeremías Berro's death. And then she would point to the candelabrum with seven burning candles behind the casket. Her gesture convinced the curious to give up and join one of the little groups chatting in the kitchen. Though she looked sunken and exhausted from a lack of sleep, Jasibe, enveloped in a dark, shabby dress, felt it was her duty to maintain ongoing respect for the memory of her husband. It had been that way for generations. Despite betrayals, deceptions, and tricks, matrimony—sanctified by God until death do you part (and beyond)—surely possessed some transcendent quality even when the spouses were unable to detect it. Maybe it was the overwhelming bond of kinship that involuntarily took shape and grew over the years. How else could you explain it?

So-called love, bodily seduction, that first bit of ecstasy. They were nothing compared to the almost incestuous genealogy that blossomed between two married people. Trivial things, all in all. Nothing to equal the solid weight of the iron link, the yoke joining two oxen as they sowed the same field. It was Jasibe's misfortune to lose that wayward brother, that child-man, that Jeremías Berro she had been promised to and saw for the first time on the day before their wedding.

When Jeremías Berro looked through his casket and saw Jasibe's insistence on such a strict observance of ritual, with so many relatives and neighbors in attendance, he smiled in death. And he remembered what had happened the night before at Alcira's wedding, how those fateful events had brought them to this moment. Alegre Carmona was there among the bridal guests. He looked older and more preoccupied than Berro could recall and the mere sight of him unleashed a powerful urge to wreak a little havoc at his expense. Though they avoided eye contact, the two men were immediately aware of one another's presence.

Carmona's sad demeanor automatically caused Berro's natural exhibitionism to become more exaggerated: he showcased every glass of anisette with a toast so boisterous, Carmona would have to acknowledge his noisy happiness all the way across the patio. For his part, don Alegre simply lowered his eyes and looked at his feet, remaining soberly indifferent to the conversations at the head of the large table where they had seated him, feeling every fiery swallow assault his throat, like a slow dagger slashing his insides.

But as soon as his right hand made contact with the silver handled carving knife resting on the poultry tray, something stirred within him. Just a vague sensation, impossible to describe, having something to do with how perfectly the knife fit into his palm when he picked it up. As though the instrument had been made for that very hand. When he grasped it in his fingers, they vibrated against the cold burnished metal. It was the first time a common household object—a table knife—had ever become something holy.

Suddenly Jeremías Berro's stentorian laughter rose above the din of overlapping conversations and forced its way into his ears. It was as though every other noise had suddenly disappeared and the hypocrite's voice was flooding the entire place. With the knife in his hand and hatred poisoning his brain (that ill-starred desire to correct God), don Alegre sat there, paralyzed, subject to a strange—soon to be uncontrollable—confabulation of desire and disdain.

They told him later, much later, when they were reading him the testimony given by Isaac Silvera, Abram Abadi, and Matilde Lofez, that he (yes, they were talking about him) had plucked the infamous carving knife from the poultry tray and with narrowed eyes, slowly walked across the patio in a diagonal line until he reached the table where Jeremías Berro, unaware of his presence, was brandishing his glass, hurling revolutionary slogans at those present, and paying homage to absent heroes nobody knew.

The witnesses stated that don Alegre Carmona stopped right at Jeremías Berro's side, but to no effect. Berro droned on and never even turned his head to notice him. Carmona waited a reasonable length of time, as though expecting a sign. A signal. Then, when his nemesis bellowed the fatal words of a new toast—"To a God who doesn't exist, and if He does exist, no one cares"—don Alegre Carmona raised the knife and held it right in front of Jeremías Berro's face, flashing it directly before his eyes. At that moment Berro seemed to awaken from a dream. He noticed a difference in the air—an inordinate silence, the mesmerized faces of his table companions—and started to rise. As he slowly stood up, the knife moved downward. Gripping the dagger, Carmona's fist descended. Its curved blade was pointed straight at Berro's heart, or more precisely, the left side of Berro's heart—the site of all his evil, his meanness— where it abruptly buried itself in one clean stroke.

Suspended between shock and incomprehension, Berro watched the blade sink into his chest as though it belonged to someone else's body. During the single second between the knife thrust and the out-pouring of dark blood that had kept him alive for more than five decades, he silently examined the silver handle and small expanse of blade jutting from his flesh. There were people standing over him. He saw their faces, transfigured above his body, as he began to fade. There was nothing to be said; words vanished from his brain. Mute, he concentrated solely on dying.

Afterwards, he saw a human figure walking toward him from a flat, infinite horizon. As it came closer, Berro experienced a growing sense of weightlessness. The figure turned out to be a very tall man, practically naked. His sealskin loincloth exposed a gaunt body barely covered by brown skin that contrasted sharply with the ash-colored beard on his face. The man stopped about four paces away and re-peated a story Jeremías used to hear as a child, a tale told to him by his grandmother Julieta, who had lived in Aleppo a century earlier.

The strains of her voice could be heard in the tall man's utter-ances: "Long ago, somewhere in the Orient, there was an old per-fumer who created aromatic elixirs. One fine day the Caliph of Per-sia, immensely wealthy but profoundly miserable because he was incapable of experiencing any joy in life, sent an emissary with an order to prepare a perfume that would transform him into a happy man. If the perfumer succeeded, he would be made as rich as the wealthiest noble. However, failure would mean execution.

"Faced with such a drastic proposal, simultaneously honorable and terrible, the perfumer worked day and night investigating the re-lationship between aromas and happiness. He studied with the pas-sion of someone on the verge death, someone who searches desper-ately for the answer that will save his life. Finally, one night, just as the Caliph was running out of patience, the perfumer appeared at the palace with a small violet flask in his hands. Pajama-clad viziers ran to awaken their ruler. Disquieted by all the commotion, the eunuchs closed the shutters of the harem, where the women, alarmed by the prospect of a happy master who could get along without them, found it impossible to sleep.

'Here is my elixir,' said the perfumer, trembling before the imposing monarch. 'It will only make you happy if you promise to smell it each time you sense the presence of death, and on no other occasion.' Surprised, the Caliph promised to try it out under the conditions stipulated by its creator.

"Days went by. Weeks. Every night the perfumer feared the Caliph's henchmen would show up at the door of his workshop to take him to his execution. Until, at the end of several months he began to think they wouldn't be coming at all. One morning he managed to obtain information from a palace servant who came to the market in search of spices: the Caliph had finally turned into a happy man. Apparently, each one of his daily anxieties brought on the feeling that death was near; so whenever he experienced this dread he followed the perfumer's instructions and opened the tiny flask. Instantly the intense aroma of spring flowers would inundate his senses and produce visions of paradise, such that the mere fact of being alive in this world seemed a privilege.

"'What did you put in that flask?' the servant wanted to know. 'Just water,' responded the perfumer. 'The aroma and the visions are produced by the Caliph's own need for happiness.'

"'Please come in,' said Angela Tejera when she saw the raw-boned, poorly clothed man with his shadowy face half hidden by a woolen scarf (unnecessary at the beginning of summer). He was carrying a floral wreath: painted wicker covered with several concentric rings of red and white carnations surrounding an enormous yellow sunflower.

"'I come in the name of the fatherland,' the stranger announced to the mourners without introducing himself. 'It's impossible to detail everything we owe to this exalted man,' he said before the shocked faces framing the unvarnished rectangular casket. 'The future will reveal more than I can today.' And spinning on his heels, he snapped to attention in front of the remains of the deceased. Then he saluted and brusquely disappeared.

"Years later they learned that this strange fellow was the very person who had acquired don Alegre Carmona's textile business when it was sold for a song, shop assistant included, at public auction."

✳ *thirty-four* ✳

FOR THIRTY CENTURIES in the once magnificent city of Ur, oft-repeated legends predicted Nazira's Mualdeb's death in her attic room on Ituzaingó Street in Montevideo. The annunciation involved the pregnancy of a black princess from the Niger, inseminated by the spirit of a minstrel who lived back in those ancient times and could make his golden harp play the loveliest melodies ever heard by human ears.

When Ur awoke to the third millennium of its now extinct epoch, it was a resplendent market filled with lapis lazuli, bronze, alabaster, and cedar wood from distant climes. Through one of history's strange paradoxes, it was ruled by a male god named Moon who conquered a female deity called Sun, the patron spirit of the nearby city of Uruk. According to the legend, one day the African princess would give birth to a beautiful tike with citrine skin and emerald eyes, whose voice, inherited from the minstrel, would forever sing litanies of consolation to those in despair.

That very same day though—thanks to heaven's remarkable sense of proportion, which always translates into the persistent impossibility of having everything all at once—somewhere in the world, a wise old woman, several hundred years old, would cease to exist.

The day Nazira died, Angela Tejera, attended in her room by Melo, the silent, black folk healer, gave birth to the child who was the fruit of her union with Carlos Gardel. The infant was well formed, with citrine skin and huge green eyes, and his first sounds weren't cries but dreamy yawns. The midwife quickly lit a green candle to appease jungle spirits and enslaved grandparents. She prayed for a long time in strange languages, her guttural voice surging up from deep inside as though it were rising from the underworld. "How odd," thought Angela, "there was almost no blood when the baby arrived." And from then on, everything would be different and newborns would enter a pristine world.

Nazira had already prepared three amulets for the day of the baby's birth—a diminutive blue crystal eye with a steady, watchful pupil, a delicate gold-filigree hand with five fingers aligned against evil spirits, and the tiny indigo blue pouch containing a wire that was twisted and tied so suffering itself would be tied up in knots and go away forever. While the midwife was placing them around his neck, she saw an empty phosphorescent silhouette that looked like a soul in transit. Though still locked in a procreative trance, Angela Tejera recognized Nazira's attentive vigilance there. And even her skirts—though made purely of reflected light—briefly acquired the consistency of plausible reality, a state with which the supernatural peacefully coexists.

At daybreak, the old black conjure woman read the kid's future in the designs made by shells thrown on the tablecloth. After the prophesy was revealed to the neighborhood women, they discussed it in secret, as is proper for miracles: the confabulation of ancestral lines that led to the child's birth would send him down paths of glory and sacrifice, failure and accomplishment. He would be a feline outcast in a world without heroes, absurd in his dignity, ridiculous in his altruism. People would not follow him while he lived, and were he to die, they would want him back. A lion in captivity.

Dragging her legs and holding in her fluids, Angela Tejera got out of bed and started making Turkish coffee as though her life depended on it. Into a narrow, single-handled pot, pour two heaping spoonfuls of finely ground black coffee. Then add two cups of water, two spoonfuls of brown sugar, a pinch of dried anise, and heat to a simmer. Watch closely to make sure the brew doesn't come to a boil, but stays right on the brink. Then, in the singular precise instant when bubbles just begin to break the surface, turn off the flame, pour the coffee into two tiny cups without handles and distribute the foam evenly between both servings.

Now Angela hears cups tinkling softly against enormous wrought-bronze trays that top a small café's stunted tables. Located somewhere in the old market of Sa-ha in Aleppo, the place bustles with people who talk and laugh as they consume thick coffee and steamed delicacies. Nazira Mualdeb sits directly in front of her—on large upholstered pillows arranged over the stone floor. Crimson silk from China encircles her jet black hair and frames the pleasant face that smiles at a steaming cup of coffee. A barefoot youth approaches, offering to fill the *narguile* next to the table. Nazira nods her head and he pours boiling water into the large glass bottle which exhales the warm aroma of tobacco scented with lavender and dried oranges. Conversation revolves around the preparation of *sahlab*, a sweetened custard from nearby Tedeff.

Angela Tejera draws deeply on the pipe and inhales a satisfying mouthful of oranges and lavender. The boy has brought a selection of small dishes—white cheese, blue olives as big as eyes, whole almonds, sesame—and a bottle of *arak*. Happiness is that ineffable thing that floats over the table and weaves itself into the smoky arabesques of conversation. A promise of summer fills the air as the sharp Levantine sun comes in through the open windows. Outside, on the immense patio of the *suk*, dozing camels, freed of their burdens, but still tied to one another, sit on the ground and dream of nocturnal caravans traveling through the remote hills of Nan Shan.

❊ *thirty-five* ❊

"PLACES AREN'T LOCATED at their sites," thought Lunita Mualdeb, now nearing the districts surrounding the port. "They dwell inside of us." Salty air blew through the intersections and filled her throat as she hurried along on a listless August afternoon. The key tucked into the pocket of her leather bag was too big and heavy to sit there without extra support, so she twirled it in her slender fingers. At the street corners, sudden gusts of wind tangled her hair. Flagstones and heaps of rubbish formed long battlements on either side of the pavement.

Suddenly she saw that façade: the double wooden doors, the black iron knocker about to pull loose from its mountings, the tall window covered with grillwork (the only one with a view of the street), its shutters hopelessly jammed shut and hanging from tracks that no longer existed. She stood in the narrow street's chilly air, her hand trembling as it palpated the key tucked away in her purse. Silence shrouded the rest of the locked houses. Some appeared to be empty. Others had metal curtains sealing their windows and in the Sunday morning light looked long abandoned. But she had a crude legacy and a key.

"Places take root in our own solitude, like premonitions, like condemnations," thought Lunita as she put her key in the rusty lock. The door groaned on its frozen hinges and a streak of light split the darkness that shrouded the remains of the tiled vestibule. She entered the house as though returning to a shy cloister, dodging small piles of trash, crumpled newspapers, the remains of old chamber pots eaten through at the base by ancient feces, fragments of what had once been chairs, sideboards, tea tables, and lace-trimmed linens. At times a dark satin shoe, crushed by years of small catastrophes, evoked a human presence, a certain radiance.

The patio—turned an eerie green by sparks from rotting garbage—seemed to move upwards to the highest heavens. In the kitchen she found gray rats who stopped in their tracks when they saw her, their red eyes glued to an unfamiliar presence. The bathroom was now a black pit that penetrated deep into the earth and vomited up insects with huge wings, creatures who collided with one another in blind flight. All that remained of the stairway was one feeble, twisted iron post, waywardly ascending toward the disintegrating upper floors, caked with the dust of their own crumbled walls.

Just then she came across the cellar. It was still down there, though its door was gone. The steep little wooden stairway protecting so many secrets had also disappeared. Lunita lit a match and held it until the flame pricked her fingers. On an impulse, she pressed her legs together and jumped down, giving in to fear and curiosity all at the same time. Then she struck another match and entered the cavern. Shattered panes in the old skylight let in the whistling ocean breeze and a few bright rays. The devastating view from the threshold would stay with her for the rest of her life. Crusty cubicles lay scattered all over the floor. At the far end of the room there was a knot of enormous ringed worms, their long bodies completely intertwined, a writhing mass, heads indistinguishable from tails, inexorably joined together, devouring one another. A nest of heteroclite reptiles slithered around and through what had once been a family skeleton: the bones still retained enough order to mimic a human form—maybe Peralta's—resting against the promontories of rubbish.

She dropped the match, and retracing her steps, climbed back up to the first floor. As she again traversed the roofless patio littered with chance residues of the past, she thought she heard soft music from a piano—a rhapsody or a serenade—something she herself had once played. And footsteps seemed to fall in the rooms upstairs, as though someone were rising out of bed and getting dressed. She envisioned round green grapes, their taut skins shimmering with tiny drops of moisture, a whole pile of grapes held in the concave expanse of her own palate, awaiting the moment when she would close her jaws. Everything foreshadowed the savory explosion that was about to flood her mind: juices inundating the interstices of her unbearable nostalgia and bathing the torn membranes adrift in her mouth. An intense warmth slowly descended to her stomach, tracing its contours and burning her insides with excessive sweetness. The grapes exploded as her molars pressed down on their sugary, gelatinous, quivering larval pulp.

Outcroppings of debris murmured phrases in a mysterious language. Realizing they were alive and whispering about her, she hastened to the vestibule where a sudden aroma of garbanzo beans and rice tried to detain her. Lunita stepped over the scraps, the remains, and tried to open the rebellious door. It refused to budge. Calling on precedented strength, she pulled the knob with both hands and broke off the bolt, which made a germinal din as it tumbled down into the sunken stairway. The door swung open and a full ocean gale blew across her face. She exited quickly, almost running, and left the cave's façade behind her, torn from her being, pulled out by the root.

She was two blocks from the sea and a heavy rain glazed the deserted promenade. Waves curled over the pink granite breakwaters like the giant tails of lacustrine monsters. She thought she could see blue mosques and minarets in the distance. Quiet chanting, intimate psalmodies filled her ears. "Places are perverse prisons," said Lunita Mualdeb. "They invade the very marrow of your bones." And she hurled the key with the same Hellenic motion that once sent a discus to the outermost limits of the earth. The key floated in the turbulent whirlwinds for a moment and then spun around on itself like a top—gracefully, elegantly—finally falling straight down into the middle of a sea that cried out like a shattered soul. It was a prolonged, desperate shriek, like the howl of an animal, and had never been heard in that place before.

TURN PAGE FOR
BAR CODE